# PRAISE FOR TRACEY TILLIS'S
## *FLASHPOINT*

"Tillis does a masterful job of combining suspense with romance and succeeds in producing a compelling, swift-moving story that features a strong, determined heroine."
—*Library Journal*

"A remarkable contribution to African-American romance fiction . . . a keeper for anyone who enjoys a sizzling romance blended with suspense, intrigue, and murder."
—*Gothic Journal*

"Well-crafted romantic suspense."
—*Minneapolis Star Tribune*

"Incorporates sizzling romance into riveting mystery."
—*Black Caucus Newsletter*

"Highly entertaining . . . promises many hours of reading pleasure."
—*Lake Worth Herald*

# FINAL ACT

## TRACEY TILLIS

AN ONYX BOOK

ONYX
Published by the Penguin Group
Penguin Putnam Inc., 375 Hudson Street,
New York, New York 10014, U.S.A.
Penguin Books Ltd, 27 Wrights Lane,
London W8 5TZ, England
Penguin Books Australia Ltd, Ringwood,
Victoria, Australia
Penguin Books Canada Ltd, 10 Alcorn Avenue,
Toronto, Ontario, Canada M4V 3B2
Penguin Books (N.Z.) Ltd, 182–190 Wairau Road,
Auckland 10, New Zealand

Penguin Books Ltd, Registered Offices:
Harmondsworth, Middlesex, England

First published by Onyx,
an imprint of Dutton Signet,
a member of Penguin Putnam Inc.

First Printing, February, 1998
10  9  8  7  6  5  4  3  2  1

REGISTERED TRADEMARK—MARCA REGISTRADA

Printed in the United States of America

PUBLISHER'S NOTE
This is a work of fiction. Names, characters, places, and incidents either are
the product of the author's imagination or are used fictitiously, and any
resemblance to actual persons, living or dead, events, or locales is entirely
coincidental.

BOOKS ARE AVAILABLE AT QUANTITY DISCOUNTS WHEN USED TO PROMOTE PROD-
UCTS OR SERVICES. FOR INFORMATION PLEASE WRITE TO PREMIUM MARKETING DIVI-
SION, PENGUIN PUTNAM INC., 375 HUDSON STREET, NEW YORK, NEW YORK 10014.

To Damon and Betty Jean Roberts,
you guys are the best.
Couldn't really have understood it
without you.
Thanks.

# PROLOGUE

---

**March 1995**

She was dead. Shannon knew it the moment the door slammed two floors below her in the foyer of her brownstone. The edge of the curtain she held away from the study window slid from her fingers to flutter against the glass.

Outside a storm raged. Inside, her stalker had come for her.

*He moved deliberately through the dark house. How could she! A flash of lightning threw the ground-floor staircase into relief. He approached and started to climb.*

She was trapped, cornered inside this elegant room while he was somewhere out there. Hunting her. *"Divorce him, bitch, if you want to live . . . Divorce him, or you'll pay."*

His threat replayed itself in her mind until the words dissolved beneath a torrent of rain that pounded against the house. *"You won't listen, will you? Fine, I'll take you out of Peter LaCrosse's life myself."*

A prolonged quiver of lightning and brutal clap of thunder shook the single reading lamp illuminating the room. Shannon watched it flicker and go out. More lightning guided her through the darkness back to her oak writing desk. She yanked open the deepest drawer and shoved her hand to the back, frantic to grip what fear had driven her to hide inside.

*He stalled at the second-floor landing, listening. She was somewhere above him. In her bedroom? Locked in a tawdry, illicit embrace? In his mind, he reread Alan's letter. His uncle said there was no doubt. He took the next stair, then the next, steadily climbing.*

The gun felt cool against Shannon's fingers. She lifted it out and released the safety.

*Her bedroom door was ajar and he approached it with dread. At the threshold, he nudged it open, found no one. Maybe —*
*But he remembered the letter.*

She doesn't love Peter. She never did, any more than she loved you. Now she's brazen. She plots on the phone with her lover while Peter is away. They laugh at him, call him a foolish old man, plot to cuckold him right in his own house.

They've planned to meet while he's out of town on business. I know you don't want to believe this but you must. Peter has to know. He won't believe me alone because he knows I distrust Shannon.

Corroboration must come from you. If you don't believe these things, go to the house and see for yourself what his wife is. She's not the woman you thought you loved. She never was.

She's a liar, a schemer, and, if you'll have the courage to see, an adulteress. We'll tell Peter together after you go to the house. Go to the house . . .

*Destroying the letter hadn't destroyed his doubts. They had to be upstairs. He turned away from the bedroom.*

What was he *doing*? . . . Then Shannon heard his measured tread on the last flight of steps. She raised the gun, steadied her breathing, faced the door.

*He could hear her now, moving inside the study. Her lover had to be in there with her. At the door, he bumped a table and swore as sharp pain flared in his thigh. Then he wrapped his hand around the brass doorknob.*

Shannon gasped when the vase in the hallway shattered against the parquet floor. More thunder assaulted her. When it receded, a broad shape stood silhouetted inside the doorway.

She fired. The man staggered and fell. Shannon stopped breathing. Then he groaned.

An awful chill washed over her and with a terrified "Ah" she let go of the gun. There was something horribly familiar . . . She dropped to her knees to touch him.

"Shannon—help me!"

She drew back in shock just as the lamp flickered back on. God, *God*, this was no killer. "Jeff!" she cried, fearing it was already too late.

She slid her arms under his shoulders and cradled his heavy body, mindless of the blood soaking her robe. "What are you doing here! It was supposed to be *him*." His stunned eyes glazed into an expression of shock and sadness; Shannon's overflowed with tears. "Don't die," she whispered. *"Please."*

But he did as she watched his chest rise and fall a final time. Her stalker had lied to her. Had his telephoned threats always been hollow, as the police had cautioned? More nuisance than menace, as Peter had warned? Was the tragic proof lying dead in her arms?

*No*, dammit. She had *believed*. Her stalker had menaced her, harassed her for weeks for the explicit purpose of making her trust his threats. And she had. Now an innocent man's life was the price.

She set Jeff's body aside gently and never remembered later how she made the awful call. She only knew, as emergency sirens approached from the distance, that she would never find a way to reconcile this. How could she live with what she had done?

And when the police pounded on her door downstairs, a worse realization overtook her. How could Peter, her dear, gentle husband, who trusted her so implicitly, ever forgive this horrible tragedy?

Despite their love, despite their lives together, from this day forward he would think of her as a killer, Jeff's killer. The murderer of his only son.

# PART ONE

PART ONE

# CHAPTER ONE

*May 1995*

"Will the defendant please rise?"

Shannon stood. The federal district courthouse was suffering from broken air conditioning and extreme summer heat, but she only felt numb and cold.

Federal District Judge Harrison Bartoly consulted the case documents before him while his clerk read the charge. "In the case of the United States of America versus Shannon LaCrosse, the defendant is charged with the crime of first-degree murder. The state contends that on the evening of March 15, 1995, Mrs. LaCrosse with premeditation and the intent to commit bodily harm shot and killed Jeffrey Pierson LaCrosse. How do you plead?"

Shannon glanced at her counsel and friend, Marshall Baker. As she waited for his answer, she wished she could borrow some of whatever emotion kept his face so impassive for this arraignment.

"Counsel?" Bartoly prompted.

Shannon's attention shifted to the bench. How did she plead? The only way she could in the wake of this terrible mistake. "Not guilty, your honor," Baker said. Shannon heard his words and involuntarily felt the weight of Jeff's lifeless body in her arms. The rage that had filled her then overwhelmed her now. She gripped the edge of the table so hard her fingers trembled. *Why*, Jeff? Why did you have to die?

## June 1995

Assistant U.S. Attorney for the prosecution Harlen Proctor leveled a long, serious look at Shannon, then at the twelve members of the jury. Calmly, he pushed away from the prosecution table and strolled over to the jury box.

"Ladies and gentlemen, the accused you see sitting before you is charged with the premeditated crime of shooting and killing her stepson, Jeffrey Pierson LaCrosse. To this shooting, she has already conceded guilt.

"What she denies is that the unfortunate taking of his life was deliberate. She denies that the taking of his life was anything other than self-defense, a horrible accident that happened when she mistook him for a stalker she claims was out to get her.

"Now in response to that claim, the prosecution asks you to consider just one very simple question. Where is her stalker? *Who* is this stalker? Where is the tangible evidence that supports, beyond a reasonable doubt, that his actions inspired a terror so great that the accused was driven to her alleged act of self-defense?

"In the absence of a concrete identity for, or act of aggression from, this invisible stalker, the accused had no need to buy a gun, hide it from her husband, then use it in an alleged panic of mistaken identity.

"Yet, according to the defense, this is precisely what happened. But unlike the defense, ladies and gentlemen, the state will present for you a more plausible case for why Shannon LaCrosse shot her stepson.

"A series of witnesses for the prosecution, re-spected men and women in this community, will paint another picture of Shannon LaCrosse. They will tell you of a woman whose intimate relation-ship with her stepson predated and lasted during her marriage to his father.

"These witnesses will present for you dates, events, and occasions—all corroborated—upon which they observed a relationship that supports a long-term affair the victim, Jeffrey LaCrosse, had with his stepmother. You'll hear how LaCrosse, driven to a state of emotional desperation by his inconstant lover, was on the verge of revealing their affair to his father. An affair about which he was conveniently silenced by his lover before he could talk."

Proctor studied the jurors' faces. Some looked him in the eye, inviting him to continue. Others looked away uncomfortably over at the defense table, glancing at Shannon.

"The question before you, then, will be this: Was Shannon LaCrosse really the unfortunate victim of terror, driven to a desperate act that night, as she claims? Or was she the calculating woman who knew exactly what she was doing when she invited her stepson to her home to talk him out of exposing her and, failing that, silenced him in a fit of rage?

"I and the defense will ask you to consider carefully, because either the vindication of—or justice for—a a dead man hangs in the balance of whatever you decide."

Marshall Baker glanced at Shannon, took in her pallor and overall brittleness as she sat rigidly beside him. He touched her cold hand. "Shannon, I know this is hard, but you have to have faith. Remember that they have a series of character witnesses who, at best, can only testify and speculate about what they think your marriage to Peter was, about what they assume they saw between you and Jeff in its aftermath.

"The prosecution's case is circumstantial. We have indisputable documentation from officers of the law. We'll see whose case holds more weight with the jury—a bunch of witnesses who arguably have emotion-based reasons to be biased against you, or the impartial testimony of the law."

Shannon listened to Marshall's words, appreciated the logic that shaped them. Still, she couldn't breathe past the fear around her heart. "I know, Marshall," she said, barely able to concentrate on what he was saying or anything that distracted her from the case the prosecution was about to put forth.

Early into the trial, Harlen Proctor called Betty Morris to the stand.

A short, heavyset woman just shy of fifty, she looked at Shannon coldly as she passed the defense table. When she was seated on the witness stand and sworn in, her nervous attention settled on Proctor.

The prosecutor smiled at her, obviously attempting to help her relax. "Mrs. Morris, could you please state your relationship to the defendant?"

"Yes." Betty cleared her throat when her soft response failed to reach the jury. "Shannon LaCrosse is married to my brother, Peter LaCrosse. My husband, Parker Morris, is Peter's corporate attorney."

"In an earlier deposition, you stated it's your belief that Shannon LaCrosse, formerly Shannon Crosby, married your brother for his money and the material luxuries he could provide her. Is that your contention today?"

"It is."

"And why do you believe that?"

"It's no secret to anyone that Peter purchased the land she wanted for a community center. Just as it's no secret to me she went after him because she knew he was rich and vulnerable enough to let her youth and beauty seduce him."

"Objection, your honor," Marshall Baker stated. "The witness is speculating on her brother's motives as well as on what may or may not have been going on inside my client's head."

Judge Bartoly gazed at Betty. "The witness will answer only the questions put directly to her. Continue, Mr. Proctor."

"Thank you, Your Honor. Now, Mrs. Morris, you've stated in earlier testimony that in addition to marrying your brother for his money, you believe Shannon LaCrosse was unfaithful to him early on in the two years they were married."

Looking at Shannon, she replied, "Yes, I did."

"On what basis did you form that conclusion?"

"I witnessed her infidelity with my own eyes."

Shannon leaned into Baker. "She's lying, Marshall. That isn't true!"

"Calm down, now. We have to hear her out before we can contradict her."

Shannon knew he was right and settled back, hating the unfairness of her sister-in-law's accusations. Where was the woman *getting* this from? She stole a glance at Peter, who sat in the front row of court spectators. What must all of this be doing to him, when he had already lost his son?

Proctor said, "Mrs. Morris, would you please clarify your allegation of Mrs. LaCrosse's infidelity?"

"I was visiting my brother four months ago when I saw her kissing another man right there in my brother's house."

Proctor let the image soak into the collective

mind of the jury. "Mrs. Morris, surely you'll agree that a kiss in and of itself isn't damning. Perhaps the kiss you witnessed wasn't a romantic embrace, as you imagined it to be."

"I'd agree with you if she hadn't been letting the man she was kissing fondle her, and if he hadn't been swearing his love."

Proctor glanced at the jury. "And who was that man, Mrs. Morris?"

Betty Morris's stern facade softened. Tears filled her eyes. "The man she was kissing was Jeffrey LaCrosse, my nephew, the man she killed. Shannon LaCrosse was having an affair with my husband's son."

Baker stood. "Your Honor, again the witness is speculating. She cannot know unequivocally that my client was cheating on her husband or carrying on in some illicit encounter with her stepson."

"Oh, yes I can, Your Honor!" Betty Morris jumped to her feet and turned to Shannon. "I know it because Jeff confessed to me before he died that he was in love with her!"

"Your honor—" Baker objected.

"What's more, she enticed him into becoming her lover, otherwise why would the man—why would *any* man—carry on like a lovesick puppy two years after she married his own father, an act that put her morally out of reach?"

Bartoly pointed a finger at Betty. "Mrs. Morris, I'm going to ask you to calm yourself and sit down or risk being held in contempt."

"Hold me in contempt, Your Honor, because before I leave this stand I'm going to tell everyone here the truth. Shannon LaCrosse seduced Jeff, just like she did my brother. Then when she got tired of the boy, she saw his devotion as an embarrassment. More than that, she saw it as a threat to her meal ticket if Peter found out."

"Your Honor—" Baker objected angrily.

"So she broke it off the only way she could. She made up this whole story about being harassed by some phone stalker so that she'd have an alibi the night she lured Jeff to the house to shut him up for good."

The court observers and reporters murmured freely, excited by the show Betty Morris was giving them. The jury sat stunned but obviously constrained to a noncommittal silence by the rules of the court.

Incensed, Baker insisted, "Your Honor, this woman is irrational. I demand she be dismissed from the witness stand and her wild remarks stricken from the record."

"Yes. Mrs. Morris—"

"She shut him up by killing him!" Betty gripped the railing in front of her and leaned toward the defense table. "You shot him. And now you have the audacity to lie to this courtroom, to lie to your husband, to insist you thought you were shooting a would-be killer in self-defense. I *hate* you for it!"

"Deputy, escort Mrs. Morris from the stand and out of this courtroom," Bartoly ordered. "Ladies and gentlemen of the jury, you will disregard Mrs.

Morris's last remarks. This courtroom will recess two hours for lunch, during which time I hope we all will regain a little decorum and"—he fixed a displeased glare on Harlen Proctor—"professionalism."

Shannon sat stunned in the face of Betty Morris's tirade. She couldn't think in the wake of such venom from the woman she'd thought was her friend. And what did she mean that Jeff had confessed his love for her?

Dear God, she thought she and Jeff had reached an understanding long ago, long after she'd made it clear to him that it was Peter with whom she'd so unexpectedly fallen in love.

And yet, Jeff had continued to care. She hadn't really realized. Or had she? Oh, Jeff . . .

*Summer 1994*
"Happy anniversary, darling." Peter LaCrosse placed a slip of paper into Shannon's outstretched hand. "You can open your eyes now."

Shannon did and gazed down with surprise and consternation at the check that lay in her palm. The monetary figure was significant and, not coincidentally, commensurate with the cost of the land she still needed for her center. Her dream.

"Peter, you promised you wouldn't do this," she told him quietly. "I told you I'm going to raise the rest of the money I need on my own."

Peter LaCrosse reached across the sitting room sofa to pull Shannon toward him. "What I promised to do was not furnish the complete balance you need for construction. I never said anything about not helping you out with the land deal."

Shannon sighed. They'd gone this round before, too often, in fact, for her to believe that another battle was going to gain her any headway.

One year into this most improbable marriage, and she was still amazed at how satisfying their union was. When Jeff had introduced them, she never could have imagined that his father would succeed in capturing her heart where the son had tried and failed.

She'd chided herself at the outset of her relationship with Peter for wanting a father figure. But as the wealthy financier had allowed her to slowly penetrate the layers of his celebrity, she had discovered and fallen in love with a touching vulnerability she hadn't expected. He needed her in a fundamental way Jeff never would.

"I love you, Peter," she told him now, leaning back a little to hold his eyes. When he lowered his mouth to hers, she felt engulfed by a familiar sense of quiet comfort.

When Peter pulled back, Shannon burrowed against his chest. "You still haven't won extra points. I mean it, Peter. When it comes to my center, I won't accept any more money from you. I didn't marry you for that."

"I'm not trying to force anything on you that makes you so clearly uncomfortable, Shannon. I just know how badly you want this. I love you enough to want to give it to you. You can't resent that."

"Of course not." But Shannon sighed because it was his impulsive spontaneity toward her that made her self-conscious in other ways, deeper ways. She was still trying to learn how to deal with the resentment it stirred from some of his oldest friends and family.

It was particularly his stepbrother, Alan Quade, who believed she couldn't possibly have married a man twenty years older for true love.

Yet when she'd voiced these concerns to Peter, he'd told her to ignore that talk, to distance herself from its negativity. The two of them knew the truth; that was all that mattered.

And yet, her worries were roused all over again later at the wedding anniversary party Peter organized. He'd stayed devotedly by her side all evening. She adored him for it, but nevertheless found it hard to maintain her calm when Alan casually sauntered up to her.

She, Peter, and a few other guests were out on the back terrace. Peter was standing a distance away, chatting with a congressman whose opinion he hoped to sway toward financial support for a pet charity of his.

Shannon was talking to the congressman's wife about a much less weighty matter—the woman's tailor. She was still smiling at the conversational trifle when the woman drifted away and Alan materialized.

"Shannon, still here. How does it feel to have survived a year?"

Shannon turned to him, her mellow mood fading. "Wonderful, Alan. Peter and I couldn't be doing better."

Had it been anyone else sipping his champagne so casually she would have relaxed. However, Alan had made it clear early into her marriage that lowering her guard around him was far from wise.

She suspected his animosity probably had to do with the way Peter was starting to seek her input on minor business decisions. She hadn't encouraged him to do it and in some instances was as surprised as Alan when Peter heeded her advice over his stepbrother's.

Alan was the traditional strategist for LaCrosse Financial Corporation. It was clear to Shannon, even if it apparently wasn't to Peter, just how deeply Alan resented his authority being usurped.

Her brother-in-law gazed beyond her now at the others mingling around them. "Well, that's all right, then. They say the first year is the toughest. If you've made it this long, I'm sure you're set for nothing but smooth sailing ahead. Excuse me, won't you?"

"Of course." Shannon was still frowning when Peter exchanged a word with his brother on his way to join her.

"You two weren't wrangling again, were you?" he asked, handing her a fresh glass of wine.

"I never wrangle with your brother, Peter."

"Ah, yes. Alan's the heavy, right?"

"Peter, it's a party. Let's not argue about this tonight." Or give the man that satisfaction of having us fight, she added silently. Then she turned her thoughts from Quade to enjoy her husband.

Peter sighed and put his arm around her shoulder. "You're right. It's just that I love you both. I can't understand why you two continue to rub each other so wrong."

"Well, my relationship with your brother is the last thing I want to talk about now." She set her glass down on a nearby table and pulled his arms around her. "Let's dance."

They did. And laughed. And mingled with their friends late into the night. It was hours before the party wound down and Shannon urged Peter upstairs while she ushered out the last of their guests.

She closed the front door behind the last one and yawned, pleasantly tired. A final once-over of the living room convinced her she could live with the minor clutter for the night. She was passing by the sitting room on the way to the stairs when she spotted a couple of discarded plates through the open door.

She ducked inside to stack them and was just turning around when someone walked out of the shadows behind her. He pushed the door slightly before he advanced toward her.

"Jeff!" Shannon jumped. He'd materialized so quietly.

"Hello, Shannon."

"You've made yourself scarce all night," she chided. "I don't think I've seen you more than twice, and that was briefly. Let's talk."

Genuinely glad to have a few moments with her friend, she reached out to give him a companionable hug. When she would have withdrawn, Jeff held on, tugging her tightly against him.

Shannon tried to pull back, belatedly realizing he had been drinking. "Jeff, what are you doing?"

"You know what." He pressed his lips lightly to the soft hair just above her temple.

"You don't want to do this," she told him, worried.

"You're wrong, Shannon," he murmured. "I do want to do this. I've wanted to for months, but you haven't let me." His hands dropped to the narrow indentation of her waist and squeezed softly. Shannon's hands followed, trying to divert his.

Shannon thought she heard a noise outside in the hall, but Jeff spoke, catching her attention. "Shannon, I love you." He resisted her attempts to push him away.

She turned her head, trying to avoid his kiss. "No, you don't, Jeff. You've just had too much to drink. Now let me go before you do something you're going to regret."

"I won't let you go." He lifted his hands to her face to hold it still and kissed her deeply, desperately.

Shock held Shannon immobile for split seconds while she endured Jeff's kiss. She lifted her hands to his chest. Still, he still wouldn't budge and she could feel him becoming aroused against her. Panicked, she shoved him away.

Jeff staggered off balance. Shannon moved back too, upset at what had happened, more upset at how it was going to jeopardize their friendship in the morning.

Jeff, looking as if he were waking from a dream, reached out to her. "Shannon, oh, my God, what have I . . . ?" He dropped his hand and turned away helplessly. "I'm so sorry."

Shannon's anger melted in the face of his sincere regret. Before this, she'd often felt guilty at being the object of his affection when she knew returning his feelings was hopeless. But now she realized she'd only been fooling herself about Jeff, about his seeming acceptance of their platonic relationship.

How could they ever go back to the safe area his action had taken them beyond tonight? Then she realized he was saying something to her.

"Did you hear me? I said I didn't mean to hurt you, Shannon. And God knows, I never want to hurt my father. I know it's him you love, that all you'll ever have left over for me is your friendship."

Shannon searched for something to say that wouldn't hurt him further. "I don't want to lose that friendship over this, Jeff. It means too much to me."

Jeff nodded sadly. "I understand."

She struggled with an irreversible sense of loss as she watched him walk away from her.

*June 1995*

Betty Morris, sitting on a bench outside the

courtroom, stared at the floor, lost in thought. She didn't realize she wasn't alone until a pair of wing-tipped shoes moved into her line of vision. Miserable, she looked up. She disliked the pleased look on her companion's face.

"You did beautifully," he told her. "Why are you crying? Because of you, Jeff's murderer is one step closer to prison, where she belongs."

Betty shook her head and looked away, dabbing at the corner of her eye. "I always liked Shannon. I just can't believe she'd do something like this. That she'd betray Peter and then Jeff. Oh, my poor boy."

"Yes, well, she had a lot of people fooled. But sometimes there is justice in this world, Betty. The guilty don't get off and evil doesn't pay. Shannon's guilty, just like I told you. Just as you testified you saw with your own eyes."

Betty sighed. "But she looked so shocked at what I said, so hurt. What if she's telling the truth? What if I was wrong, if I just thought I saw—"

"Stop it!" He took a breath, making an effort to project the cool control she had come to expect from him, the control that governed the ruthless business tactics his enemies hated and his colleagues respected. The control that had earned him the nickname he knew they whispered behind his back: the Iceman. He relished it. "You and I and the others already concurred on Shannon's duplicity prior to all of this, didn't we?"

Betty studied his stern face, his hard eyes. "Yes," she murmured.

"And each of you knows the episodes you witnessed were the truth. And that Shannon, no matter how tragic she pretends to be inside that courtroom, is just a manipulative little liar who must be punished."

"Yes."

He smiled again. "Then don't worry about your testimony. You've spoken what's in your heart. Now let justice take its course."

On day five, Proctor called Alan Quade to the stand.

"Mr. Quade, based on your close relationship with your nephew, could you help clarify for the court what might have motivated him to confront his stepmother on that fatal night?"

Quade glanced briefly at Shannon. "His inability, I believe, to continue living with the guilt of something I discovered long ago." His gaze moved behind her to his brother. "Peter, it's for Jeff's sake that I have to say this."

Baker raised a skeptical eyebrow, commenting from his seat. "Your Honor, this melodrama is touching—"

"Mr. Quade, a simple answer to Mr. Proctor's question will do."

"Of course, Your Honor." Quade said to Proctor. "Shortly before his death, I felt compelled to pull my nephew aside for some candid advice. I told him I'd guessed of his affair with Shannon, and that it had to stop or I'd be forced to tell Peter."

"He's a liar!" Shannon whispered furiously to Baker. "Marshall!" She laid a hand on his arm, while she locked her gaze on Quade.

"Careful Shannon, the jury's watching."

Shannon restrained herself while she seethed at her brother-in-law's blatant lies.

"How did you learn of an affair, Mr. Quade?" Proctor continued.

"I simply put two and two together. Several times—at family functions, get-togethers—I observed the two of them engaged in what I can only describe as intimate exchanges."

"Exchanges?"

"Yes. My stepsister, Betty Morris, confided in me that she too had witnessed the same."

Proctor's expression was earnest. "Could you be more precise about what you both witnessed?"

Again, Quade glanced at Peter. "Lovers' touches, kisses, whispers. Do I really need to say more than that?"

"No, I think we all understand you, Mr. Quade. Thank you; I have no further questions."

Bartoly turned his contemplation from Quade to Marshall. "Do you wish to cross-examine, Mr. Baker?"

"I do, Your Honor." He walked away from the defense table. Standing in front of Quade, he said, "You've testified to seeing and overhearing these episodes you characterize as intimate. Did you ever confront your sister-in-law, face-to-face, about what you assumed you'd witnessed?"

"Shannon has always been the picture-perfect wife to my brother."

Shannon despised Quade's sarcasm almost as much as his piety.

Quade continued, "I knew that an appeal to her would be . . . meaningless." He looked out over the jury as if what he had to say next was incredibly hard.

"My nephew was very defensive when I confronted *him.* He told me he and Shannon had never deliberately set out to hurt Peter; theirs was an association that preceded her marriage.

"He told me that though Shannon had married Peter for his money and the social advantages he could provide, she sincerely hoped she could grow to love him. But when that didn't happen, she and Jeff remained lovers."

Shannon looked at the jurors to gauge the effect Quade's tale was having. She didn't see nearly the skepticism she had hoped for. And why should she? Jeff was dead. In his absence, they had only Quade's word and that of the other prosecution witnesses.

Their word was that of respected stalwarts of Washington society. Hers was of a young, relative nobody whose personal history of urban poverty still made many God-fearing citizens uncomfortable, no matter how politically incorrect their fear.

*Oh my God,* Shannon thought. She dropped her gaze to the table and her folded hands.

\*    \*    \*

"This court is in session. All rise."

Shannon responded more slowly than those around her to the court clerk. It was the second week of the trial. She felt drained, alone. Too many emotional surprises were bombarding her. Too many repressed resentments from those she and Peter had called friends were wearing her down.

Accusations kept resonating in her head . . . "Yes, Shannon and Jeff went out in public together. In fact, they seemed to have remained unusually intimate after her marriage . . . Yes, a casual touch here, a murmured exchange there . . . hadn't raised suspicions at the time, but in hindsight . . ."

In a perverse way, Shannon just wished all of their innuendos would resolve this trial one way or the other so that she could retreat and deal with the upheaval privately.

Baker, observing her distraction, leaned over and said, "Hang in there. Today we start our defense and we'll earn some points back on our side."

Shannon nodded wearily. She hoped Marshall could do it, but an odd apathy was overtaking her, urging her again to just wish for an end, whatever it might be.

That afternoon, Marshall called Jeff's former roommate to the stand. The young man testified that he had noted Jeff's distraction and agitation the evening of Jeff's death.

Jeff had been adamant about something having happened that necessitated his taking an emergency flight out of town that very night. But he'd never indicated that the problem was his family, or that his primary destination was home.

"So, as far as you know, he could have been headed anywhere, with his visit home a mere afterthought."

"Absolutely."

Shannon was buoyed to see this testimony make a noticeable impression on the jury. Obviously, they were reconsidering some simplistic conclusions the prosecution's presentation had previously helped them make.

Marshall's following witnesses were a series of police officers who had investigated Jeff LaCrosse's homicide. His main witness among them was the lead investigator, David Courtney.

"Detective, for two months, Mrs. LaCrosse intermittently filed complaints with your department about these phone threats she alleges she received, is that correct?"

"Yes, it is."

"It was her allegation that the man who harassed her threatened to take her life, is that true?"

"Yes."

"And what measures did you and your colleagues take to investigate those allegations?"

"We put wiretaps on the LaCrosses' telephones for a period of two months, the time during which these calls occurred."

"And based on the evidence those taps provided, was it your professional conclusion that Mrs. LaCrosse was telling the truth about being harassed, or was she lying?"

Courtney's eyes moved past Baker to Shannon. "She was telling the truth about receiving an inordinate number of phone calls that were sexually aggressive."

"Could you be more specific for us laymen in the court, Detective?"

"The caller barraged Mrs. LaCrosse with an inventory of lewd and obscene acts he wished to—inflict—upon her. He further suggested that he was watching her, that it was only a matter of time before he positioned himself to make his fantasies come true."

"In your professional assessment, then, he did in fact threaten actual bodily harm to Shannon LaCrosse?"

"Yes, that was my judgement."

"And Mrs. LaCrosse shared this 'judgement?' "

David smiled slightly at Baker's tone. "Yes."

"How do you know?"

"Her consistent response to the calls and verbal attacks was agitated. She repeatedly rejected the caller's threats and told him how offensive she found him to be."

Shannon released a small sigh. She held the detective's gaze for moments before he looked away and back to the lawyer.

"So Detective, the official police determination on the terrorism Shannon experienced prior to Jeffrey LaCrosse's death is that these threats were not figments of her imagination."

"That's correct."

"Indeed. And in your experience and professional judgement, could this persistent—barrage, as you put it—of phone threats have provided sufficient motivation for a woman to want to protect herself by any means possible? To arm herself against some unnamed though imminent bodily harm?"

Again, David's eyes touched Shannon's. "It could."

Baker turned to the jury. "Thank you, Detective. I have no further questions, Your Honor." He walked briskly back to the defense table.

"Mr. Proctor, do you wish to cross-examine?" Bartoly asked.

"Indeed, Your Honor." The prosecutor folded his arms over his chest and took slow steps to stand before David. A picture of contemplation, he asked, "Detective, you've outlined the degree of sexual harassment Mrs. LaCrosse received prior to her stepson's death. But I'm puzzled. In none of your testimony did I hear you say this caller literally threatened to kill her. Am I right?"

"There are implied threats, and there are literal ones, Mr. Proctor. Too often, the violent actions of a perpetrator make hindsight distinctions ridiculous, if not tragic."

"In your professional opinion."

"In my professional experience."

"However, the fact remains that at no time during any of these recorded conversations did this man flat-out threaten to kill Shannon LaCrosse. Is that true?"

David sighed impatiently. "It was precisely because he leveled a clear murder threat that Mrs. LaCrosse and her husband asked the police to monitor his phone calls in the first place."

"And yet, you never got a plainly spoken murder threat on tape. Did you?"

David hesitated.

"Yes or no, Detective?"

"No," he allowed tersely.

"Thank you. Now, the other matter that puzzles me involves a time factor. Two months into monitoring these harassment calls, the police were still unable to trace their point of origin or the perpetrator, is that true?"

"Generally, the brevity of his conversations prevented us from ascertaining a sufficient trace. Twice, we thought we had something. But followup determined the locations to be dead ends."

"Dead ends," Proctor mused. "In fact, Detective, isn't it because when after this two-month period the calls ceased altogether, the investigation into Shannon LaCrosse's harassment and alleged death threats was officially stopped?"

David folded his hands in his lap. "There are procedural rules that govern standard investigatory process. When a degree of tangible evidence cannot be obtained, or a case for probable cause sustained, an investigation is generally concluded unless further action occurs. That's what happened in this case."

"In other words, with no more calls, no persecutor, and nothing else concrete to go on, you were procedurally compelled to shut the investigation down."

"That's correct."

"Given the virulence of this harasser's verbal aggression, did you not think it odd that he would suddenly cease all contact with Mrs. LaCrosse?"

"Your Honor, Mr. Proctor is asking the witness to speculate," Baker objected.

"Sustained. Rephrase, Mr. Proctor."

"Detective, in your professional experience, is it usual for someone who makes such explicit and unrelenting threats of sexual aggression to suddenly drop all contact with his victim?"

"Sometimes, what you're dealing with is a smokescreen, very carefully constructed by a perpetrator to obscure what is actual fact."

"But nothing between the time the calls stopped and Jeffrey LaCrosse's death suggests such was the case with Shannon LaCrosse's caller. In fact, one might even conclude that these calls, the ones you got on tape, conveniently followed the actual death threats we'll have to accept on Mrs. LaCrosse's word. These elusive calls would support the panic alibi Mrs. LaCrosse insists drove her to murder her stepson."

"Objection, Your Honor!" Baker barked, rising.

"Sustained. Mr. Proctor, be careful."

"I have no further questions for this witness, Your Honor."

The Iceman listened to Proctor's words while he watched Shannon LaCrosse's face. She looked devastated. His eyes turned to Proctor. The counselor seemed confident and the Iceman could guess why. The cop's no-nonsense testimony had been effective, as far as it went.

A reasonable motivation, supported by documented phone logs, for Shannon's state of mind when she'd shot Jeff had been presented. But thanks to the Iceman's pretrial intervention with key witnesses, the more provocative question had become, was her motivation fact or a fabrication devised by an adulteress out to silence her lover?

Poor Shannon, he thought, studying her again. He caught the faint trembling of her mouth. Excellent.

Two days later, Baker offered his summation. "Ladies and gentlemen of the jury, the phone records supporting the threats Shannon LaCrosse feared do exist. As you've heard, it's a matter of public record that she did not imagine their seriousness or the very real person who made them.

"It is further fact that the prosecution's circumstantial case rests solely on a supposed affair Mrs. LaCrosse had with her stepson, its compromising consequences, and an alleged angry confrontation that drove her to murder.

"The proverbial woman scorned: That's Shannon LaCrosse, if you believe the prosecution. I'll grant you, his scenario makes for provocative melodrama. But at its core, that's all it is—drama.

"What you need to consider as you reach a decision is what's tangible, what's actual truth. Shannon LaCrosse acted as would any reasonable person who feared for her life. We know that prior to Jeff LaCrosse's death, she was hounded by an unidentified yet very real man who not only harassed her but literally threatened her life.

"You've listened to a professional assessment of what constitutes a threat, as well as a legal distinction of what does and does not theoretically justify a police investigation. But like you, ladies and gentlemen, I don't live most of my life in a theoretical world circumscribed by stern rules. Where I come from, a threat is a threat, period.

"Shannon LaCrosse is not a reckless killer. She is as much a victim in this tragedy as Jeffrey LaCrosse. For whatever sick purpose, she was deliberately set up by a faceless stranger to fear for her life. She acted on her fear in a way any one of you might have, and mistakenly took the life of an innocent man who simply showed up in the wrong place at the wrong time."

Shannon turned to look over her shoulder at Peter. She was frightened of what she might see in his eyes. When his gaze met hers and then dropped away, she turned back to the bench, stricken.

Marshall continued, "Mrs. LaCrosse has already admitted freely to having sustained a close friendship with the deceased that postdated her marriage to the deceased's father. As for the intimacy that's been repeatedly alluded to between Mrs. LaCrosse and her stepson, I can only speak for myself. I, too, tend to be physically demonstrative with my closest friends. A touch, a friendly pat, even a platonic kiss isn't out of the question.

He paused, then said, "Perhaps I, like you, have simply had the luck not to have had my innocent actions scrutinized because I made an unconventional marriage that makes me suspect in already-suspicious minds.

"That's why, based on the facts, ladies and gentlemen—the *facts* and not hearsay—there is only one responsible unanimous verdict you can reach in good faith. I urge you to make it."

Silence gripped the room after Baker sat down. Shannon tried to read Proctor. Though seemingly affected by Baker's summation, he still looked confident.

The Iceman could all but taste victory as he watched the jury recess to consider their verdict. He *felt* confident his biggest obstacle to Peter was nearly out of the way. Because of his clear thinking and fearlessness to act, the LaCrosse corporation was finally poised on the brink of real prosperity.

With Shannon out of the way, Peter would be his to influence. And he'd feel free to resume embezzling the company funds Peter's stubbornness was forcing him to steal. Once the proof of profit rested firmly in his hands, he'd reveal to Peter the deal that was guaranteed to make everyone it touched obscenely rich.

The next hours that passed seemed to Shannon like an eternity. It was late evening by the time she and Marshall were summoned back to the courtroom.

She stood stiffly beside him, bracing herself to hear her fate while the jurors filed back inside. Marshall, apparently sensitive to her fear, moved his hand to briefly touch hers.

The clerk passed the written verdict to Bartoly, who read it impassively. His calm baritone pierced the heavy silence when he asked the jury's foreman to stand. "Ladies and gentlemen of the jury," he said, "have you reached a verdict?"

# CHAPTER TWO

The jury foreman answered, "We have, Your Honor."

Shannon stared at the solemn man whose answer would dictate her future. She willed him to look at her so that she might read the decision in his expression. He kept his eyes fixed on the judge. She looked blindly down at the defense table. The judge's complicated predeliberation instructions, including the first-degree murder or lesser degrees of homicide of which she could still be found guilty, all crowded her mind in whirling confusion.

The foreman said, "On the charge of murder in the first degree, we the jury find the defendant not guilty."

An audible gasp erupted from the spectators in the courtroom. Shannon leaned heavily against Marshall's supporting arm, still afraid to trust the rush of relief that warred with her icy fear.

Bartoly asked, "On the charge of murder in the second degree, how do you find the defendant?"

"Not guilty, Your Honor."

Shannon squeezed Marshall's hand and glanced at Proctor. He looked grim as he glared right back at her.

Bartoly continued, "On the charge of voluntary manslaughter, how do you find the defendant?"

The foreman looked at Shannon and away a split second before he responded. "Guilty, Your Honor. We find the defendant guilty of voluntary manslaughter."

Shannon felt herself actually sway. Through the buzzing in her ears, she heard Marshall ask for a poll of the jurors to verify the unanimity of the verdict. Reporters erupted from their seats. Those who didn't head for the doors made a collective move, as if waiting for the chance to rush the prosecution's table.

Bartoly's gavel demanded order. "Ladies and gentlemen! It is by my discretion that your cameras are in this courtroom and it is by that discretion that I won't hesitate to throw them and you out. Now sit *down*." He waited for the reporters to comply. After most had, he said, "Sentencing will take place six weeks from now in this courtroom. Until that time, at which she will appear, the court will allow Mrs. LaCrosse to await sentencing outside of jail, yet while still in the custody of this court.

"Thank you for your patience, ladies and gentlemen of the jury. The bench fully recognizes that these proceedings have tested us all. *"Now,"* he said as he leveled everyone a heavy look, "this court is adjourned."

*     *     *

With Bartoly's departure, Shannon felt the verdict take on a finality that smothered something vital inside her. The court deputy shouldered his way through the crowd to take her into custody for processing of her temporary release. "No," she protested, and didn't know she'd spoken aloud until he looked at her sharply. Then he reached for her hands and clamped the hated metal cuffs around her slender wrists.

Baker jostled her, causing her to look at him. He was trying to keep his balance against the newshounds and shield her at the same time. He leaned down and said something against her ear.

"What?" Shannon felt frantic, dazed, unable to comprehend what he was telling her.

"I said, we're going to appeal this verdict, damn it! Don't give up, Shannon. We'll get it reversed."

"Marshall?" She tried to find the hope he alluded to beneath the angry frustration of his expression. When she couldn't, the tears she'd held back for weeks spilled down her face.

"Shannon! Can we have a statement?"

"Get me out of here," she pleaded, shrinking back from Baker, away from the cuffs, away from the crowd of reporters. She stepped closer to the deputy, preferring even his protection to the throng coming at her.

The deputy took her arm to lead her away when a voice behind them stopped her where she stood.

Shannon shut her eyes and turned. The crowd parted and grew quiet. As if of one accord, they allowed her an unobstructed view of the man who approached. Shannon felt heartsick when her husband visibly faltered.

"Peter, please." She wanted to keep this private, for their ears only. But in the deathly quiet of the room, his silence accused her, forced her to speak. "I didn't do this."

Peter LaCrosse ran a hand across his haggard face.

"Please, Peter. Tell me that at least *you* believe me."

At first, Peter LaCrosse said nothing, and then he answered, "I know you didn't *mean* for this to happen, Shannon."

But Shannon saw the grief lining her husband's face, knew it was not the emotion of a man who trusted in her innocence. "Peter, it's *you* I love." She held her breath, begging him to see with his heart that she spoke the truth. But as he continued to hesitate, she knew whatever he said would decree how she lived with the nightmare she'd inflicted on his life.

"Shannon, God help me, I . . . I can't forgive this. I can't forgive *you!*" He broke down.

The crowd whispered.

Shannon felt breathless, dizzy.

"Let's go, Mrs. LaCrosse," the deputy said quietly. The reporters clamored again. But this time they turned to Peter, scenting the promise of the more wrenching story they'd get from him rather than from the convicted killer, his condemned young wife.

Shannon's last impression as she walked from the courtroom was of how brutally the events of this nightmare had aged her husband.

But beyond that, she walked away knowing the pained accusation in his eyes was going to haunt her long into the wasted years ahead.

The Iceman savored the absolute terror in Shannon's eyes, almost as much as he appreciated the desolation in Peter's. Peter's pain was unfortunate, but the total public decimation and humiliation of Shannon had been critical. Peter had been allowed to waiver in her influence. Arnaud and the other investors had already concurred with him that they couldn't afford to continue to wait for Peter to come around in order to proceed.

And so, now Shannon was gone; not dead, and therefore a martyr whose memory would never be erased from her husband's lovesick heart. But rather, she was a thoroughly disgraced woman who had caused him the sort of humiliation and grief he would never be able to forgive or forget.

Detective David Courtney sat at the back of the empty courtroom. His chin was propped on his hand. His eyes were closed. His thoughts were racing.

The reporters had gone. The spectators had drifted away.

Was the verdict just? Had everyone who testified against her been wrong?

Dammit. Or had *he* been wrong?

\*     \*     \*

*December 1992*

The sound of the breaking bottle caught David's attention. A woman's muffled scream held it. He tucked the box of chocolates he carried under his arm and reached under his coat for his gun.

Both sounds came from an alley just ahead. Slowly approaching, David backed against a brick wall and peered around the corner to get a look. A tall, thin male, swaddled in a leather jacket and hood that obscured his face, held the point of a knife to a woman's throat.

The woman was pinned between the rear door of a dry cleaner and an overflowing trash dumpster. At her feet lay a shattered liquor bottle and a mangled bouquet of roses. David used the dark to cover his progress. As he moved closer, he heard the woman say, "Aaron, don't hurt me. You know I'm not your enemy."

"Yeah, I know. You just want to help, right? Shannon Crosby, the do-gooder who thinks she's too good for me. I been telling you for weeks, girl, how you can really help me." He moved closer. So did the knife, until it touched her skin. "Now I'm gonna show you, right here where there ain't no other counselors or cops. Just you and me. One on one."

"No," Shannon gasped, and twisted her head away when the man tried to force a kiss on her.

David moved. Shannon tried to throw a punch, but her attacker caught it. David stalled the punk's retaliation by pressing his gun right against the man's ear. His box of chocolates hit the ground.

"Get away from her," David growled, jerking the man away. "You're under arrest." Keeping his eyes on the assailant, he asked Shannon, "Are you hurt?"

"No." But her hands shook as she buttoned her coat. "Don't hurt him, Officer. He made a mistake."

David snatched off the assailant's hood. The man he held was little more than a boy. Nevertheless, David kept his gun where it was as he looked at Shannon incredulously. "Don't tell me you aren't going to press charges. This punk was about to have you for a late-night snack."

Shannon knelt to reclaim her purse, then moved away from the building until she stood right in front of the boy. She watched him while she said to David, "He was confused. This has taught him his mistake. Right, Aaron?"

"Don't go trying to do me no more favors, lady."

David said, "Listen to Aaron, lady. Maybe he's not so dumb after all."

But Shannon stood her ground, as did Aaron.

David looked from one to the other, wondering who would waver first. Surprisingly, it was the kid. He hunched his shoulders and looked at the ground. "If you gonna arrest me, cop, do it."

Since he seemed to be the only one overly concerned about the violence that had almost happened, David was finding the standoff slightly ridiculous. He turned his attention to Shannon. "What's it going to be?"

Shannon debated, then said, "He goes."

David shook his head and lowered his gun. He gave the boy a shove. "Get out of here. And don't let me see your sorry ass again."

The boy looked at Shannon one last time before he ran. David watched him, then turned to see what the would-be victim was doing now. She was back at the spot where he first saw her, trying to retrieve her flowers.

David was still a little annoyed with the entire incident, but her dejection made him walk over to her anyway. She didn't acknowledge him; she just concentrated on those damned flowers.

David shook his head and hunkered down to help. "Here, let me." He pushed her hands away. "You're just making more of a mess." Shannon glared at him. The effect was undermined by the tears in her eyes.

David pondered those tears, her trembling mouth, the faint shock he could still see by the spill of the nearby streetlight. Despite it all, he was momentarily struck by what seemed to him to be the flawless beauty of her face.

Smooth coffee-colored skin, exotically high cheekbones, dark, silky brows. Her hair, cut short as a boy's, was styled in a sleek, feminine cap. Tendrils of it kissed the delicate lines of her cheek and jaw.

What had the kid called her? Counselor? She was a lawyer. Figured. They generally displayed more sense in the courtroom than out on the urban streets of the punks they defended. In fact, this "Shannon" exuded an extra bit of fragility he found hard to reconcile with someone whose work made her rub elbows with lowlifes like Aaron.

In fact, David rather thought the counselor looked like the type who ought to be home arranging flowers instead of retrieving them from some dirty, pissed-in ally.

He restored her wilted stems to their wrinkled cellophane and handed them over. Solemnly, she accepted them with a hand that had steadied, he noticed. David salvaged his own chocolates, then helped her to her feet.

By unspoken consent, they started walking, neither talking. David wasn't sure where they were going and he was late for his date. But somehow this prolonged rescue of Shannon seemed more urgent. "My name's David Courtney."

"Yes, I know. I've seen you around the police station."

David threw her a surprised glance.

"I'm a social worker with the Department of Corrections."

Ah, *that* kind of counselor, he amended.

"I guess it's pretty obvious I'm new."

Her smile was self-mocking under the streetlights, and David nodded. "You were lucky I came along. But as you say, you're new and everybody gets suckered once." He shoved his hands inside his coat pockets, keeping the chocolates lodged under one arm. "The trick is not to repeat your mistakes. Why *did* you let that boy go?"

Shannon stopped walking. They had reached a deserted-looking townhouse and she gestured at the steps. "Do you mind if we sit, detective?"

Because the plea in her eyes contradicted her even voice, David climbed a couple of stairs and held out his hand.

Shannon took it and sat beside him, looking out over the quiet street. "You were right. I probably should have let you arrest Aaron. I . . . I guess I got sentimental and screwed up."

David leaned back on an elbow, studying her. "As I said, why?"

Shannon looked inward, weighing parallels between Aaron Robbins and a boy long dead whose name had been Joe. "Aaron isn't much younger than I am. We come from the same neighborhood, the same street.

"I knew him when he used to get into trouble as a little kid. He stole money to help support himself and his younger brothers because his parents are worse than useless, always have been. From his perspective he's never had better choices."

"So you're saying he's not really the hardcase he appears to be." David looked away from her, out over the street, too. "I don't know, Shannon. Attempted rape seems like a pretty tough crime to me."

Shannon looked at him. "I know. I also know he's lived his life in and out of the system. I guess

I had the conceit to believe I'd finally talked him into staying straight this time." She sighed. "Why would he jeopardize everything he's gained by trying something stupid like this now?"

"You're an attractive woman, Shannon."

She frowned, impatient. "You know as well as I do what happened back there wasn't about sex. It was about control and his need to exert it over someone vulnerable. Why me?"

David shrugged. "It wasn't only about sex, you're right, although that played into his motivation, too. You're a special authority figure to him because you got right up close to him, right inside his head. That makes you particularly vulnerable to him."

"I was just doing my job."

"Yes. You were pushing him to achieve, exerting *your* authority over him. Some who live behind an eight ball all their lives just need to push back. They need to remind themselves they have the power to do it, to manipulate people where *they* want them to be."

"What you're saying is, no matter how responsive a client may seem to be, I'm ultimately very foolish to get involved."

"Not involved, attached. The clients and criminals you and I deal with have had years to harden up. When we're lucky, a little of our attention and nonconfrontational words may soften their shells. But that still never guarantees they're going to turn out the way we want them to."

Shannon rested her head on her knees, pensive.

At length, David ventured, "Is he going to be awfully worried?"

"Who?" Shannon glanced at him.

"The man who earned the wine and flowers. The one you were on your way to see."

"Oh." Shannon shook her head. "I wasn't meeting anyone. The flowers and wine were for me. Congratulations from friends for a funding grant I secured tonight."

"You were on your way home, then."

"Yes. My apartment is only two streets over."

David got up. "Come on, I'll walk you the rest of the way."

"Wait a minute. What about you? Those chocolates suggest you weren't necessarily on *your* way home."

"No big deal." David thought of the woman who waited and the argument that would ensue. He thought of how maybe it was overdue and probably for the best.

Shannon continued, "I feel guilty for ruining your evening." Just then, a taxi rounded the corner. Shannon hopped down the steps to hail it. When the car stopped, she turned back to David. "I guess all that's left to say is, thanks again."

He nodded. "Chances are we'll be seeing each other around."

Shannon smiled slightly before she climbed inside.

David watched the cab for a moment, then on impulse called, "Wait!" He hurried down the steps and gestured for her to roll down her window. When she had, he handed his scuffed box of chocolates through to her. "You look like maybe you can use one or two."

Shannon accepted them hesitantly.

David smiled because she looked touched.

"Thanks," she murmured.

"You're welcome," he responded as softly, understanding.

Shannon clutched the box tightly in her lap as the cab pulled away.

"I'll be seeing you," David murmured thoughtfully as the car drove off into the cold, starry night.


The next time he saw her was on New Year's Eve. The police station was winding down with an end-of-the-day holiday party that traditionally preceded more serious after-hours celebrations. Other corrections and legal personnel who frequented the station during the day were present. Accordingly, an abundance of attorneys and social workers filled the squad room.

Shannon appeared about an hour into the party.

David caught sight of her from a distance. "Excuse me," he murmured to a colleague whose engagement he'd just toasted with a coke. He weaved his way through laughing, dancing bodies to get to her.

Shannon was chuckling at some heavy-handed flirting from the cop beside her when David tapped her from behind. She looked around and experienced an instant frisson of nerves and pleasure. "Detective. Have you turned up to rescue me again?"

David gave his colleague a bland look. "Should I?"

The officer shrugged good-naturedly and walked away.

"Very smooth," Shannon murmured. She sipped from the soft drink she was holding.

David merely smiled. She was as tailored and lovely as he remembered. He wondered if she realized just how expressive her big brown eyes were, deciding she probably didn't. If she did, she'd be running from the slow burn she kindled inside him instead of relaxing with such a companionable smile.

Shannon said, "If I had three guesses, my first would be that tonight of all nights you probably won't be standing up your date."

David chuckled, acknowledging the reference to their last encounter. "What's so special about tonight? And who says I have a date?"

"It's New Year's Eve. Don't you?"

"Do you care?"

"I'm just making conversation."

"Um-hmm."

Shannon smiled. "Honest."

David inclined his head.

Her gaze moved past him to a group of patrolmen who broke up at something someone in their group said.

"So whose yours?" David said.

Shannon turned back to his question. "My what?"

"Date."

"Do you care?"

David considered evasion, impulsively opted for candor. "Yes. I do."

Shannon sobered a little. Despite his light tone, she sensed some part of him wasn't joking and wasn't sure how she felt about that.

David added mildly, "Nothing to say?"

"Nothing I'm sure a flirt like you hasn't already heard too many times before."

David plucked a chocolate-covered cherry from a bowl resting on a table beside him. He held it close to Shannon's mouth so that she was forced to take a bite. "Don't sell yourself short, sweetheart."

"Don't you oversell yourself, period, Detective."

He winced.

"Oh, come on, you're tougher than that."

"Are you so sure?"

Shannon hesitated, then said, "Yes. I know your type."

David laughed softly and cocked his head. "Really? This should be good."

Shannon nodded, as if he had confirmed something. "That's part of it, that charming self-effacement to offset the good looks. A man of physical presence, as quick with words as he is to answer a call to action."

David narrowed his eyes. "I think I'm flattered."

"Don't be. That was an analytical assessment, supported by department gossip."

David laughed outright.

"You see, we single women are prey to speculation breathlessly volunteered by interested onlookers who just love to share a juicy tidbit."

"Onlookers. So you're saying you haven't been asking around, then." He selected another cherry and enjoyed her fluster while he chewed it. "Pity. I've been asking around about you."

"What?"

David almost smiled. "Don't worry, you're the original mystery lady."

Dangerous, Shannon decided. "You put too exotic a slant on things, Detective. I'm an open book. There isn't anything mysterious about me."

David stepped a little closer to her. "In that case, maybe I should take advantage of this chance to . . . act . . . instead of talk." He placed his hands lightly on her waist. "Let's dance."

Shannon let him pull her along. They weren't conspicuous, given the number of others moving casually to a radio someone had cranked up to help simulate a dance band. But the moment Shannon looked up into his intent golden eyes, the instant she felt his large hands encircle her waist to pull her close to his hard, rangy body, she felt strangely exposed.

The tune was up-tempo but David kept their pace slow. Again, Shannon let him. Apparently encouraged, he dared pull her a little closer.

Technically, she supposed he was taking liberties. What she couldn't understand was why she wasn't objecting.

It wasn't that she was opposed to sexually aggressive men, but neither was she in the habit of gravitating to them. Her reticence had less to do with fear than with her need to control situations that threatened to make her vulnerable.

She'd seen too many other women lose their sense of self beneath a romantic haze that exacted more from them than it returned. And if that wasn't enough, she'd learned lessons from her own past that lingered indelibly.

But she couldn't remember a temptation quite as compelling as David seemed to offer her now.

When the song ended, he didn't let her go. He took her hand. Shannon observed that no one seemed to think it unusual when he pulled her along behind him away from the crush to a closed office door.

When he reached for the doorknob with his free hand, Shannon pulled back. "Hold on, the dance was nice, but—I can't believe you want me to disappear with you behind the proverbial locked door."

With a half-smile, David turned the knob. The door swung open. "It isn't locked."

Shannon eyed him.

All innocence, he eyed her back. "I don't suppose you'd believe there really is something inside I want you to see?"

"Are you normally this big a tease?"

David's sober tone surprised them both. "I'm not kidding."

Shannon's stomach fluttered and she considered walking away.

David tugged her hand. "Come on, you're a big girl." His mouth curved. "I dare you."

It was his challenge that pushed Shannon past him and inside the room.

David followed and quietly shut the door. The frosted glass of the window pane further secluded them.

Shannon took in the name plaque on the desk of the lieutenant whose private space they were invading. She noticed the slight disarray of paperwork cluttering the utilitarian desk and the coffee cup that needed washing. She was aware of the muted party noise seeping inside the room.

Then she was aware of David, standing close behind her.

"Turn around and look," he murmured at her shoulder.

Shannon turned. Just above her head, David held a little plastic sprig of mistletoe. "I dare you," he whispered again and lowered his mouth to hers.

Shannon nearly backed away, but the elemental part of her kept her where she was. She admitted she had wondered about this since the night David had pulled her out of the alley. Now as his soft warm lips moved over hers, her uppermost thought was that satisfying her curiosity had been worth the wait.

Aside from the kiss, he didn't touch her. But she felt the impact all the way to her toes. His subtlety frightened her because she felt the control she so valued slowly slipping away. Startled, she drew back.

David read confusion in her eyes. Somehow her quiet uncertainty sparked his own. He'd expected some cool retort, had been prepared to meet it with one of his own that would keep this flirtation in its proper perspective.

Instead, he marveled at his racing heart and the glimmer of need that urged him to take advantage of Shannon's uncertainty again. He leaned into her but she raised a slender hand to his chest, stopping him.

"I didn't mean to stay at the party this long," she voiced, faintly. "It's late. I'd better go."

David pondered that. "You don't have to. Maybe . . . we could get out of here together."

He sounded so appealing she wanted—*needed*—to run. "No, Detective." She stepped around him. "I don't want to interrupt your evening a second time around."

David kept his back to her, hardly seeing the cluttered desk he was staring at. He was seeing Shannon as she had been on another winter's night, a little shaken, a little alone, very beautiful to him. On this night as on that one, she was someone he very much wanted to hold.

That self-awareness alone shaped his quiet response while she walked out the door. "Happy New Year, Shannon."

*    *    *

Three months later, he encountered her again.

He was standing at the cash bar inside the ball-room of a pricy commercial waterfront complex. Idly watching the crush milling around, he found himself preoccupied not with the community service award he was to receive, but with thoughts of Shannon. Again.

What would have happened between them if they'd thrown their reservations to the wind that New Year's Eve night?

He set his glass down on the bar, impatient to shake off her memory. And suddenly she was there, standing right across the room.

She hovered at the entrance registration table, unescorted and stunning in a simple blue silk suit. For the first time, David carefully scanned the pro-gram in his hand. There at the bottom, scheduled for honorable mention, was Shannon Crosby, the chief Ernst Street Community Center developer and coordinator.

Feeling suddenly as if the evening had acquired real promise, David weaved his way through the crowd.

Shannon saw him coming. The particular inner jolt she'd begun to anticipate whenever she saw him kept the smile at someone's casual comment on her face while she tensed at his progress. She'd noticed his name on the program moments ago and been surprised and unsettled to find him here.

Given the recent turn her life had taken since she'd last seen him, she was uncomfortable with the inevitable awkwardness the evening promised.

"Shannon, you look beautiful," David said as he reached her. He took her hand and gently squeezed it, distracted by the flicker of apprehension she couldn't hide.

He glimpsed an empty table at the back of the room and headed for it. The romantic view of moonlight through the terrace doors beyond seemed ridiculously appropriate for what he wanted to say.

Once they were seated, David just gazed at her for a moment, trying to see beyond her beauty, needing to understand why everything about her had the power to overshadow that of every other woman he'd been spending time with lately.

He signaled a passing waiter to order wine and in the interim silence, studied her bent head.

"Shannon, you have to know I'm attracted to you. I have been since that first night we met."

Shannon's eyes lifted to his, then she looked back down. "Well, that's direct." She fingered the fragile stem of the crystal glass their waiter had placed in front of her.

"You can't honestly tell me it comes as a big surprise to you."

"No. Honestly I can't."

"Then why are you sitting there so distant, as if we were complete strangers?" He reached across the table to touch her hand.

Shannon gazed at him for a long time. "Our

timing is—off, David. My reasons are that simple."

And that complex, he thought, wishing she would articulate what was behind her pensiveness. He frowned, preparing to push when another voice interrupted them.

"Shannon, here you are." Peter LaCrosse walked around the table to stand behind her chair and placed both hands on her shoulders. Then he leaned down to kiss her cheek.

David looked first at the celebrity financier, then at Shannon. She didn't back away from the question in his eyes. Hers even seemed to hold a faint apology.

"Detective, have I had the pleasure?" Peter LaCrosse asked quietly.

Since LaCrosse already knew he was a detective, David mused, obviously he had already had the pleasure from someone other than him. "No, But your reputation precedes you, sir. It's an honor."

The man had made a fortune as a city builder. David knew LaCrosse had earned an equal fortune in national respect by rechanneling much of what he made into charities and local social causes. He extended his hand to the older man.

Oddly, LaCrosse seemed to breathe a little easier as he took it. In that moment, David realized LaCrosse was disconcerted, too.

"David's something of a hero to a lot of disadvantaged kids around this city, Peter." Shannon reached up to clasp the hand LaCrosse kept on her shoulder. "He's been building a reputation of his own. That's why he's here tonight, to be recognized."

"She exaggerates," David murmured, figuring out the dynamics here. LaCrosse had to be considerably older than Shannon. Yet he was clearly being proprietary, which suggested intimacy.

"You're being modest," Shannon said.

David shrugged, distracted. "Lots of guys are Big Brothers. I just happened to be the one singled out tonight."

Maybe, he decided, he had simply wandered into one of the oldest scenarios in the book. A beautiful young woman chose the rich, older man over the enamored but outranked suitor.

Involuntarily, David's eyes dropped to Shannon's mouth. For a split second, he felt its softness as she surrendered to him. When he raised his gaze back to hers, he saw her breath catch before she looked away.

David pushed back his chair. Second fiddle had never appealed. "Will you two excuse me? I don't want to intrude."

He supposed the twinge of satisfaction he felt at the annoyed flash of Shannon's eyes was immature. Then again, he decided his reaction was okay when LaCrosse's hands tightened around Shannon's shoulders.

David shifted his attention from that contact to meet LaCrosse's look. Unexpectedly, the expression on the older man's face softened just when David expected smugness or even condescension.

Well. Maybe he should be consoled that Shannon's winner at least appeared to be a class act. "LaCrosse, Shannon," he nodded, and left the table.

### June 1995

"Why are you still here, man?"

David opened his eyes. The shadows around him were deepening outside the windows, lengthening across the courtroom floor. The room was completely empty now, except for his partner, Jack Martinez, who dropped into the seat beside him.

"In case you didn't notice, the show's over," Jack said.

"Why is that, exactly, Jack?"

Jack shrugged. "What do you mean? Shannon LaCrosse is guilty. A jury of her peers said so."

"Yes, they had to find her guilty of something, didn't they?"

"A little tense, aren't you?" Jack said after watching him for a beat.

David sighed. Jack was right. Dammit, why couldn't he pinpoint the source of his impatience?

"Listen," Jack began, "I know you had a thing for Shannon LaCrosse—"

"I did not have a 'thing'."

"All I'm saying is that I know you're not indifferent and the lady is beautiful. But the truth is, she got bored with her old man, got the hots for his son, and initiated something she couldn't handle in the end. Old song, old verse."

"That's so easy, Jack. Didn't you ever wonder

just once why all of this—the motive, the set-up, the crime—all played out like clockwork?"

"Come on, we both know some of the most meticulously planned crimes go off like clockwork. That's what happened with Shannon LaCrosse and her stepson. They got careless, she got impatient, then she got unlucky."

Yeah, David thought. Had he done all that he should have to make sure that was the truth, to ensure that slick plotting on her part was all that was involved here?

"You hungry?" Jack got up and dug his keys out of his pants pocket. "There's this little place me and Marie discovered off Pennsylvania."

David heard Jack, but he couldn't get Shannon or the verdict out of his mind. Maybe his partner was right. Maybe he'd just never cooled down from a two-year-old memory of an attraction that had unexpectedly tempted him to want more.

He followed his partner outside into the twilight, remembering Shannon's vulnerability, the honest awareness of him she hadn't denied even when she was choosing LaCrosse.

Could that same woman have turned into the reckless schemer convicted here today?

Even if the answer was yes, she'd never impressed him as being stupid. Why would she make such a fatal slip now?

Oh, get a grip, Courtney, he told himself as traffic broke, allowing him to dodge the next onrush to get to his car.

As he pulled away from the curb to follow Jack,

he concentrated on maneuvering through the stop-and-go congestion surrounding him.

Jack was right. Shannon LaCrosse had been declared guilty. His men's investigation—his own contribution to the case—had been thorough. The manslaughter verdict was tragic.

But it wasn't wrong.

# CHAPTER THREE

*December 1996*
*Brewster Correctional Facility, Washington, D.C.*
Shannon hovered on the edges of sleep, fighting the dream. It fought back, relentlessly determined to have its way.

She threw an arm over her eyes to mute the ever-constant glow of prison yard lights that filtered intrusively into her cell tonight as on every night. She tossed on the thin mattress that taunted her memory of comfort from a life that seemed increasingly remote. And then, a pitiful whimpering two cells down pierced the night's silence to assault her senses.

The new inmate on the block could have been her, *was* her not so long ago, when she'd finally realized she wasn't getting out of here.

The new girl started to sob. Shannon wanted to feel pity, but her eyes remained dry. That stranger's sorrow was an unwanted siren call to fears she'd spent a lifetime suppressing, only to be resurrected in this place. And now that girl's tears, and the hopelessness of confinement, were drawing those fears painfully out.

The night pressed on, imposing its own special desolation on time that already hung too heavily in this place. Shannon's eyes finally closed, but her subconsciousness listened avidly to the new girl and remembered . . .

"Shannon, run!"

Her eyes locked indecisively onto her fourteen-year-old brother, Joe. He hovered impatiently at the front door, willing her to do as she was told. But she couldn't, not while their mama was weak from the dope she'd taken. Shannon tightened her arms around her mother, who lay shivering on the floor. "Joe, we *can't* leave," she pleaded.

"We can. She's dead, Shannon."

"*No!*"

"Come *on* before the police come get us, girl!"

Defiantly, Shannon pulled her mother closer. She braced her thin back against the wall to ease the cramps in her legs.

One of the neighbors probably had already called the police, just like the last time her mother and the new boyfriend, Howard, had fought. Just like then, they'd been screaming at each other. But this time, when her mother told Howard she loved him, he shoved her until she fell hard against the floor.

Shannon, a cringing witness as usual, had run to Howard while he screamed down at her mother. She had used her small fists to stop him, to make him go away and leave them alone. But

Howard had only retaliated as he usually did when his lover was too sick to defend her child.

He had grabbed Shannon's thin arm hard enough to make her fear this time he'd break it. Then he had dragged her to the living room closet and locked her inside.

She cried and pleaded for him to let her out. But he hadn't, because he never did. So she'd slid to the floor, trapped inside the terrifying block of darkness.

She'd sat there trembling, unaware of the point at which she'd stopped hearing her own sobs. All she'd known were the four walls of her prison closing her in. And Howard, still yelling, before the awful scuffling sounds of him hitting her mother began.

Forever passed before he finally slammed out of the apartment and Joe came home. Her brother heard her renewed cries and threw open the closet door to let her out. He'd looked like an angel to her despite the fury and tears that darkened his young–old face.

Now he was ordering her to run with him, to run away from their lives.

"Baby!" Shannon looked down at her mother, who was barely managing to whisper her name. She *was* alive.

"Mama, you've got to get up." Shannon tried to scramble to her feet, to lift her mother with her.

"Shannon, dammit!" Joe stared at her from across the living room door.

She ignored him and continued to pull.

"No, Shannon stop." Joycelyn Davis used the last of her strength to resist her daughter. "Go on with your brother, baby."

Sick with anger all over again because her mother wouldn't help her, Shannon leaned close to catch the faint words uttered with a desperate breath.

"Ain't nothin' here for you no more. The cops ain't got nothin' for you 'cause they lie. They don't care. Nobody cares, so you've got to look out for yourself." She lifted an unsteady hand to grip one of her daughter's. "You hear me! Take care of yourself first. *Always*. That's how you're gonna stay *alive*."

"Mama, please . . ." But her mother's hand dropped away and her head rolled back against Shannon's chest.

"Girl!" Joe shouted.

Shannon carefully wiped away a thin line of spit that trailed from her mother's slack mouth. Joe's voice seemed to recede to a distance. Tenderly, she rocked her mother until everything around her began to ease into a strange, comforting calm. To Joe, she said simply, "Mama's dying. We can't leave."

Joe yanked Shannon away from the dead woman. "You can't help her, *nobody* can help her. That shit Howard gave her finally killed her this time."

Shannon stared at him, not comprehending.

Joe grabbed her shoulders and shook her.

"Stop it," she mumbled, trying to push him away.

"No, I won't stop it until you listen to me." He shook her harder. "Listen!"

Shannon felt the calm start to lift. Fear seeped in to take its place. She whimpered, trying not to cry.

"You and me are each other's only family now," Joe said harshly. "You hear me? When the cops come, they ain't gonna care about that. All they gonna do is hustle us out of this apartment and force us to live with people we don't know. You want that? To live without me, all alone?"

Miserable, sobbing after all, Shannon shook her head. "Don't go, Joe!"

Joe dragged her to the front door and threw it open. "Come on, then."

Shannon caught a glimpse of a gun shoved under his jacket. "The cops are gonna leave us alone," he muttered just before they started to run.

Shannon spared her mother a last look before Joe hauled her into the hallway. Her last memory was of a robe hiked up too high on thin thighs scarred by needle tracks.

They ran. Neighbors opened their doors to see what was going on. When Joe showed his gun, they slammed them shut again.

Shannon and Joe hit the first floor landing as the shriek of sirens bled through the door.

"Joe?" she whispered, uncertain.

This time when Joe touched his gun, he pulled

it out. "Stay with me," he ordered, and he shoved open the door.

Shannon stumbled at their brutal pace. Joe righted her and she ran as hard as she could, trying to keep up. Joe headed for an alley Shannon knew bordered his friend Juney's house. She'd realized long ago it was with Juney's gang that he lived more than he lived at home.

Shannon felt herself tiring when, suddenly, people around them started scattering. Her heart slammed when she heard a cop shout behind them, "Police! Stop where you are, kid and drop the gun. *Now!*"

But Joe didn't stop. He twisted Shannon around while they both moved. And then Shannon screamed, her ears ringing and going numb. Joe aimed his gun and squeezed off another shot at the cop.

The cop began cussing just before she and Joe started running again, full-out.

"Joe, stop," she pleaded. She didn't want to get shot and die.

"Shut up!" Joe kept running.

"Let the girl go. Drop your gun, boy!"

Shannon looked over her shoulder. Two cops were chasing them now, instead of one. Both had pulled their guns.

"*Joe!*" she begged, pulling on his hand to slow him down. She tried to pry his fingers away, then abruptly, Joe let her go. She fell, crying out when the hard sidewalk scraped her knees. She looked up just as Joe fired over her shoulder and took off.

People all along the street were in a panic now. Some of them were screaming, but she couldn't understand them because her eyes were locked on her brother. He was getting away—and then he went down.

Shannon heard the shot when Joe fell on top of his gun. His body jerked once before he lay unmoving.

She screamed and scrambled to her feet to get to him. He was on his stomach, one arm caught beneath him while a puddle of blood pooled under his jacket.

"No," Shannon cried, putting her arms around him, trying to drag him up. "Don't, don't . . ." And then someone touched her shoulder, started to lift her away.

"Come on," the cop said. "He's gone."

Shannon used her open hands to lash out. "I hate you, I *hate you!*" The cop grabbed her arms and pushed them down to her sides.

She shook and hiccupped for breath while more cops arrived. All of them huddled around Joe. The one who held onto her pulled her over to a parked squad car.

"No," she whispered when the door slammed behind her, shutting her inside. She hugged herself, chilled to the bone despite the summer humidity. "No, *no.*"

Joe was gone. Her mother was gone. She was alone and her mother had warned her. Nobody would take care of her. No one would care.

The squad car pulled away from the curb and she began to cry. But she didn't look back.

"You have a visitor, princess."

Shannon came awake with a start. The glare from the prison yard was gone, replaced now by the gray glow of a rainy morning's light. Her heart was still racing.

She lay motionless, feeling remnant dream tears wet her face. She forced herself to take slow, restorative breaths, as had become her habit. Nothing else had the power to neutralize the horrors of the past.

Gradually, she turned from the wall to face the guard who had summoned her. The woman looked sullen, as usual. Shannon closed her eyes again. "Who's my visitor?"

"Your husband."

Shannon's heart thudded this time for a very different reason. Reluctantly, she slid her feet off the bed.

She hadn't seen Peter face to face since the day she'd been sentenced to five years of this hell. He'd made it clear that he couldn't bear to look at her, let alone live with her for the few precious days of freedom she'd been granted by the court to get her life in order before she began her incarceration.

"You got thirty minutes with him." The guard backed out of the cell and Shannon frowned at the instruction that had sounded more like a taunt. Thirty minutes was all she'd ever had.

While other inmates were granted an hour, she was not because that extra time was one of many little privileges denied her as a prisoner living under protective custody.

The court, concerned for her safety because of her local celebrity status, had ordered protective custody during her term. And though the order was meant to safeguard her, it felt more like intolerable isolation with each passing day.

She saw no one except her guards and she ate with no one. She talked with no one, except for one or two loyal friends from Corrections who weren't too uncomfortable to visit each month. And of course, her adoptive family visited, but the experience was so painful for them all she almost wished they wouldn't.

Shannon stared at her cell door, wishing now she didn't have to open it, didn't have to face Peter. The tiny space confined her, but it also sheltered and right now she needed extra minutes of privacy to prepare herself for what surely was going to be an ordeal.

She sighed, letting that wish, as she had so many other hopes, go. Living in here had taught her that the smoothest path to the least resistance was to simply do as she was told.

She got off her bed, wishing she had a real mirror instead of the tiny square bolted to the cinderblock wall above her dingy commode. Her eye fell on the metal locker that was her closet. She felt no joy at selecting attire from the blue standard-

issue cotton pants and smocks that constituted the
extent of her prison wardrobe.

God knew she hadn't been born with much. But
the system had helped her get her life on a track
that had allowed her to take for granted the simple comforts of life.

What would Peter think of this place, with its
iron doors and timed buzzers and armed guards
who glared mistrustfully at the visitors as well
as the inmates? More importantly, she thought,
swallowing, what would he think of her now that
she was one of those inmates, forced to consider
this place her home?

She picked up her comb and ran it through her
hair, noting absently how it had grown. She lingered over her image in the mirror. Not exactly
the glamorous woman the media had once
courted. She didn't miss their attention, but it was
more than depressing to know that little about
her appearance these days would even begin to
interest it.

With no reason left to stall, she told her guard
she was ready to go.

Inside the visitation room, Shannon sat behind
the barrier of plexiglass that separated the inmate
and guest phones. She was contemplating hers
when the opening of the outer door brought up
her head. She watched Peter being escorted inside.

He hesitated and she saw his cautious expression give way to pity and something else. Re-
morse? She hoped so, for abandoning her.

Peter sat down and picked up his phone.

Shannon did the same.

"Hello Shannon. You look . . . good."

"I look like hell. Why did you come, Peter?" Why *now*?

Peter's eyes flickered but he held her gaze.

Shannon wondered if he deserved points for fortitude.

"It's Christmas, Shannon. Let's not fight."

"Is that what this is, then? A mercy visit?" Her pride stung while he just sat there, his startled expression seeming to indicate he thought she should feel comforted.

"Your solicitude is about one year too late, Peter." Now he looked sad, but Shannon remained unmoved. She didn't deserve her husband's pity for an offense she hadn't committed.

"Shannon, my coming here is about more than that." LaCrosse touched the glass between them.

Shannon merely followed the gesture with her eyes. She was seeing beyond the glass, beyond him, remembering how he'd literally turned his back on her after the trial. "You're right, Peter. Let's not fight." She pushed her chair back, ready to cut his penance short.

"No, please, Shannon! I *miss* you."

It was the declaration she had longed to hear. But now that he'd actually voiced it, she felt strangely distant. Still, she sat back down and picked up her phone. "How can you mean that, or even say it when you refuse to believe me?"

This time, LaCrosse groped for an answer.

"Shannon, I've told you, I know you never intended to hurt me or my son."

Never *intended*? Shannon flinched at the simple brutality beneath her husband's earnest declaration. When she could speak, she said, "Well, I guess I should thank you for that."

Peter stared at her intently through the glass. "I still love you."

"How can you if you believe I'd betray our marriage vows, especially with your own *son*?"

"I don't know, Shannon, but I—"

"Do?" she supplied bitterly. "You think I slept with Jeff." She wanted to comfort him and hit him at the same time. She glanced at the clock on the far wall. Minutes left. Part of her was glad while another part of her wanted to cry.

She was as surprised as Peter appeared to be when a tear did slip down her cheek.

"God, Shannon, don't."

"Why not?" she demanded, anger exposing the injustice of her situation. "Crying is one of the few actions I retain control of in here. Can you imagine what that's like, Peter? How pathetic, that is, because it's so true?"

Peter closed his eyes and whispered, "I'm so sorry. I can't *stand* to see you hurting like this."

"You're a hypocrite," Shannon shot back. "You say you miss me, but you think I'm sitting exactly where I belong. After all, your friends warned you something bad was bound to happen when you entangled yourself with me."

"Shannon, that's not fair! I married you, didn't I?"

She knew he hadn't meant to be callous. Then again, maybe he'd only voiced precisely what he'd always subconsciously thought. She signaled for the guard.

To her husband, she stated quietly, "I won't stay to remind you of your mistake." She got up and walked away.

"Peter, talk to me; you look miserable." Alan Quade glanced questioningly at Parker Morris, who leaned against the mantle on the far wall of LaCrosse's study. Morris shrugged. Quade carried his coffee across the firelit width of the room and seated himself on the sofa beside his brother's chair. "Your visit with Shannon didn't go well?"

"Alan, how in the hell could something like that go 'well'? It was torture for us both."

"If you anticipated that, why did you go?"

Peter looked hard at Quade. "What kind of question is that?"

"An honest one. She killed your boy. How could you want anything to do with her after that?"

LaCrosse snapped, "You were hardly her greatest fan, Alan, even before all this. You can't understand."

"I never hated Shannon, Peter. I just didn't trust her. She's a young, beautiful girl, bright, driven. She had her whole future ahead of her and what did she do? I know." He held up a hand at Peter's sharp look, "she fell madly in love with you and agreed to marriage, despite the literal world of difference between you."

"Age never mattered."

"Yes," Alan nodded. "Actually, I saw that almost immediately after you two said your vows. That's why it was all the more painful to watch her affections shift."

"She was never unfaithful before."

"Brother, we're both men of the world. These things happen, no matter how innocently the parties involved start out. Like you, I'll never believe either Jeff or Shannon intentionally set out to betray you."

"That wasn't your position after the shooting."

"I was distraught after the shooting. We all were, we all said things that probably deserve to be forgotten."

Morris left the mantle to sit beside Peter. He clasped his hands then looked intently at his friend. "The truth is, your wife, no matter how innocently, fell into an affair with your son. For whatever reasons—perhaps Jeff was the first to exercise the sense to try to pull away, who knows?—she ended it badly. And now she's in prison serving her time for it."

Peter raised his hand to massage away a vague discomfort in his chest. He saw his brother catch the gesture and aim a narrowed, concerned look at him, questioning. Peter quickly dropped his hand. He also considered what Parker had just said. Despite everything, he still loved his wife.

Which finally decided something he'd been struggling with for a long time. Maybe too long. As Parker pointed out, Shannon was in prison. He'd be damned if she stayed there much longer.

It was nearly ten p.m. when LaCrosse punched in a number on his bedside phone. Marshall Baker picked up on the third ring.

"Who is this?" Baker demanded huskily.

"Peter." At the ensuing silence, LaCrosse added, "I've disturbed you."

"But you aren't going to hang up."

Peter sought a response.

Baker sighed. "Hell, wait a minute."

Peter heard him murmur to someone before he came back on the line. "All right, I'm all yours."

"I've been thinking about Shannon."

"Yeah. Actually, so have I lately, a lot. This will be her second Christmas in that place."

"I saw her today, Marshall."

"That must have been rough," Baker said carefully. "For both of you."

"You have no idea."

"You're wrong, Peter, I do. She doesn't belong in there."

"I know. I'll never believe she wanted Jeff dead."

"Never believe she wanted—? Dammit, Peter, was that the best you could give her? You really believe she's guilty, don't you?"

Agitated because he was unable to categorically dispute his friend, Peter insisted, "I could never have loved her if she were the heartless monster the jury convicted."

"Yet you can't get past the thought of her and Jeff together."

"I don't know why the hell I called you."

"Don't hang up!" Baker sighed. "I just can't understand how the two of you, when you had so much going for you, could have come to this."

"Maybe it was inevitable, Marshall. Shannon is young but she was never blind. Jeff was a very attractive boy."

"Bullshit. That sounds like Quade talking."

Defensive, LaCrosse said, "Sometimes the obvious speaks for itself."

"Yeah, sure."

"Listen, I didn't call to rehash what's done. I called because of what has yet to be done. I want Shannon's investigation reopened. I want her out of that place."

"You know I've filed an appeal."

"Yes. But even you can't hold out much hope that her conviction will be overturned. The evidence against her was convincing. The opposing character witnesses were persuasive. The police records supporting our claims of harassment, while they existed, weren't. I can't believe our chances are good."

"We can't know that, Peter."

"Can't we?"

"It'll be tough," Baker allowed.

"Maybe impossible. That's why I want you to talk to the police again. Get something more solid that will prove Shannon's assertion of self-defense."

"I can't manufacture evidence that isn't there."

"No. But you can initiate a search for something that's been neglected. What about those phone records taken from the wiretaps? There has to be a way to get more from them, to get the case reopened, justify another investigation."

"Listen to yourself, Peter. You're not talking like a man who believes his wife is an adulterous murderess."

LaCrosse ignored that. "Find a tangible connection between the police records and Shannon's stalker. Find him, Marshall."

"Courtney." David tucked the phone receiver tighter between his ear and his shoulder.

"Detective, my name is Marshall Baker."

"Yeah?" David straightened a set of reports he was organizing against his cluttered desk.

"I was Shannon LaCrosse's defense attorney."

David's hands stilled. He laid down the papers. "Yeah."

"I need your help."

David waited.

"Shannon's case shouldn't be closed. I believe there's unfinished business to it, something perhaps you're in the most likely position to resolve."

"Why?"

"Shannon told me you two knew each other before all of this happened."

"We were little more than business acquaintances."

"Before or after LaCrosse came onto the scene?"

"Get to the point, Baker."

"Shannon shot Jeff LaCrosse, mistaking him for a killer against whom she had to defend her life. You practically conceded that in your testimony during her trial."

Idly, David followed the progress of a janitor across the hall. "Besides the routine advocacy she hired you for, why are you so hot to dredge all of this up again?"

"This isn't about me. Shannon LaCrosse's history with this community and the people she was committed to help won't let it rest."

"Saint Shannon," David murmured.

"What about you, Detective? Is there some reason for your sarcasm, or are you just naturally a bastard?"

David glanced at his watch. "Meet me in one hour. At Tim's."

"Fine. I'll see you then. Thanks."

"Don't thank me yet."

David deliberately arrived ten minutes early. Recognizing Baker from the trial, he spotted him at the back of the room. He also took a moment to size Baker up, unobserved. The drinking crowd was fair for a Friday night as he weaved his way through small clusters of tables to the bar. He needed the bartender, whose eye he caught.

"David, man. Been a long time since you've wandered in here on a Friday night."

David's smile was quick, though not particularly inviting. "I'm wondering about someone, could be a regular. Marshall Baker."

Ed set a beer down in front of a middle-aged businessman. "I know him."

"Tell me."

"Marshall's not actually what you'd call a regular, but he lights here often enough for me to recognize him when he comes through the door." He gestured beyond David's shoulder with his chin. "Back table, to the right."

David nodded, his smile genuine this time. "Baker," he said when he reached the lawyer's table.

Marshall Baker raised an eyebrow. "Ed seemed pretty chatty from where I'm sitting."

Still smiling, David pulled out a chair. A pretty young waitress smoothly materialized. David ordered beer, delaying conversation with the lawyer. Habit had him shifting his chair to observe the room.

Presently, Marshall leaned across the table to make himself heard above the pub noise. "Let's get something straight up front so that we won't waste each other's time. Why are you so reluctant now to believe in Shannon's innocence?"

"I'm here, aren't I?"

"Under some duress. In fact, if you hadn't proven yourself during the trial, I'd say you're carrying the attitude of a man bearing a grudge."

# CHAPTER FOUR

David's smile faded, along with his indulgent mood. "The LaCrosse investigation was tight. Shannon LaCrosse's defense boiled down to her word and tears against LaCrosse's corpse. The dead man spoke louder."

"Only to those who weren't listening to Shannon."

Defensive, and irritated for feeling that way, David demanded, "What's your next question?"

"You haven't answered my first one. Why are you still against Shannon?"

David sipped his beer. "I'm not against her; I never was. The fact is, I called in some favors to get a couple of my guys cruising the LaCrosse house after the department stopped the investigation. They watched out for anything suspicious. Nothing ever turned up."

Baker thought, not until Shannon's stepson came home for an unannounced visit when he should have been on a plane, on his way to do business. He leaned back in his chair. To give Courtney his due, he hadn't expected the news about the surveillance. "How long did you guys watch her house?"

"Long enough to determine that this stalker was probably going to be more mouth than anything. When his harassment stopped, I couldn't justify continuing further surveillance."

"But you and Shannon were friends prior to this case," Baker insisted, trying to reach the man beyond the cop. "Didn't you ever consider circumventing the rules because of that alone?"

That was the heart of the question David still wrestled with. He searched deep inside himself for an honest answer.

Baker continued, "What if I offered you an incentive, unofficially, to make a little more off-duty digging worth your while?"

David eyed the lawyer. "You could be sliding onto dangerous ground, Counselor."

"Then dammit, tell me what ground I need to break. What will it take to get through to you?"

David studied Baker. "What's your real stake in this?"

"I already told you. An innocent woman's life."

"That's all?"

Baker narrowed his eyes, trying to understand the question, trying to read David's neutral expression. When understanding dawned, he smiled, not in the least amused. "One extramarital affair balanced against a full plate of social obligations would probably overtax even the average woman, Detective. Make up your mind. Either Shannon LaCrosse was screwing her stepson or she was screwing me. I seriously doubt she would have been cheating with us both."

David had regretted the insinuation even before it left his mouth. He finished his beer. "All right. Here's the deal. I'll put some of my own time into a follow-up. When I'm through, we'll have it all or nothing. But whatever turns up is going to resolve this thing once and for all. Agreed?"

Baker watched Courtney's eyes. "Okay. You give it your best shot and we'll call it done."

David dug some bills out of his hip pocket and laid them on the table. "I'll be in touch." He stood.

"Courtney?"

David waited.

"Thanks."

He inclined his head.

"And Detective?"

David turned a second time.

"Shannon would thank you, too."

After the door closed, sealing the noise of the bar off behind him, David found himself bypassing his car. He blended in with a number of other pedestrians out to stroll. It was going on six o'clock, which meant the tourist crowds from the trolleys were pretty much dissipating for the day.

Georgetown regulars and business commuters idling around to catch a meal or a drink before heading home to suburbia kept him company while he walked.

He found himself turning onto a street of stately old brownstones. Home wasn't a destination he made the time to visit often these days, at least not beyond the obligatory monthly check-ins and holidays. He found himself headed there now.

The narrow red door that distinguished his parents' house greeted him as it had every day during his childhood, with subtle wealth and grace. His father, a career diplomat, had made the decision long ago not to settle in amidst the exclusive ranks of his colleagues around Embassy Row.

Rather, he'd fancifully embraced this older, more classically structured community for the sense of home it gave him.

David's earliest recollection was simply that the house and neighborhood had been his first significant stomping ground, his safehouse.

He pushed open the gleaming wrought-iron gate that enclosed the small, immaculately groomed yard. Wanting to prolong his temporary solitude, he indulged what had been a favorite habit as a child. He sat on the stoop and, despite the cold, let the calm night air wash over him.

This was the best kind of evening to seek counsel with one's own thoughts. Despite the area's popularity with the tourists, night sounds were settling around him into an exclusive hush that was old and familiar.

Marshall Baker had no idea of the strength of the nerve he'd hit when he'd given him a hard time about Shannon. But then, with the exception of Jack, who was only aware of some of it, no one *knew*.

David reached down and picked up a small

stone. He turned it over in his hand. The final night he and Shannon had met hadn't been unlike this one. Perhaps that similarity was rousing unwanted memories now.

On the other hand, maybe facing them was the best way to make peace with them.

It had been two weeks after his encounter with her and LaCrosse at the waterfront party. David had been leaving the station, headed home, when he'd noticed Shannon standing alone beside the water cooler in the hallway.

As he'd studied her quiet dejection, every instinct had urged him to keep walking. But he'd heard talk of the hard time she'd been having with one of her younger clients, a boy whose incorrigibility had pulled him firmly out of her care and into the hands of the law.

Any good cop who had ever wrestled with the unique frustration of weighing duties to the system against the emotionalism of the job understood what she had to be feeling. He'd found himself detouring.

"David!" Shannon crumpled the paper cup she held and tossed it into a nearby trash can. "I didn't hear you."

"I didn't mean to startle you, you just looked . . . Do you need anything?"

She tilted her head, questioning.

"Surely you don't still need to be here. It's late."

Shannon's expression cleared. "Actually, I was just leaving."

Yet David noticed she seemed reluctant to go.

Her hesitation should have been *his* cue to go. "Headed anywhere particular?"

Shannon shrugged. "Just home." She turned so that they stood side by side as they started to walk. "You?"

"Some of the guys are hanging out at a joint around the corner."

Shannon nodded.

David sensed he was making a mistake but continued talking anyway. "Listen, neither of us seems in a hurry to go anywhere. How about letting me buy you dinner?"

Shannon concentrated on the faded tile floor while they walked to the door.

David knew she was considering. And she'd already made her involvement with LaCrosse clear. No matter how vulnerable the lady seemed, he was ultimately wasting his time.

"Where did you have in mind?" Shannon finally asked.

David let the exit loom closer. "I know a place northwest of here."

Twenty minutes later, they were locking up his car and Shannon was pondering the marquee above the restaurant. "Ben's Chili Bowl," she mused.

"You know it?" David held the door open for her.

"Know it? As a kid I lived it, just like everybody else around here. I was just thinking I've been away too long."

David smiled, appreciating her whimsy. All the

way over, he'd reminded himself this wasn't a date. But her intimate tone couldn't stop this isolated moment from feeling like one.

Inside, Shannon took a stool beside him. She gave the counter clerks, the long shotgun interior, the diverse patrons an appreciative look. David scanned the menu boards on the wall over the grill. Some of them, he knew, had been in place more than forty years.

He ordered them each the house specialty of loaded dogs with fries. While they were waiting for the food to come up, he glanced at Shannon and caught her tentative smile. He threw in two chocolate shakes. The hell this wasn't a date.

They carried their food over to one of two empty booths lining the wall. David noted the framed news clippings over their heads were at least twenty years old. Each captured a moment in time when a famous entertainer, sports figure, or city celebrity had stopped by to share a bite with the local clientele.

Shannon commented, "You know, it's odd how trendy this place has become. I remember when it was patronized almost exclusively by the blacks in the neighborhood."

David nodded absently, wondering if he should reach over to brush away the drop of chili sauce that dotted her mouth like a beauty mark.

"I guess that's all kind of academic to you since America isn't your original family home," she said.

David curled his fingers around his sandwich, instead. "How do you know that?"

Shannon smiled. "Sources."

"Which ones?" David pressed, more curious than annoyed. He wanted to hear why she would have made the effort to dig out that information. She most certainly would have had to have made an effort, since he didn't routinely discuss his private life around the office.

"Your partner, Jack. We were having a casual discussion one day about one of my kids. He told me you'd had a run-in with the boy's brother back when you were new on the force. One question led to another and Jack mentioned that this territory was a far cry from your ancestral neck of the woods.

David didn't realize his annoyance showed until Shannon said seriously, "Don't be angry with Jack. I pushed, and he was just being a nice guy."

She was right. His life wasn't a big secret. It was just that since in so many ways his childhood had been public, he protected his privacy now as an adult. "I'm not angry."

"So, what about it?"

"What about what?" David picked up a fry, ran it through a pool of ketchup on his plate.

"Your European roots, private school, the whole privileged thing. How in the world did you ever become an inner-city D.C. cop?"

"Funny, that tone of dismay. You sound just like my mom."

"I'm serious."

"So am I."

Shannon encouraged him with a raised a brow.

"Okay, the short version. My dad is British and my mother is African. Ethiopian."

Ah, Shannon thought, that explained his golden skin, the amber eyes, his exotic good looks.

"They met in London while they were in college. My dad's father was a career diplomat and my dad was studying to follow in his footsteps. My mom was an economics major. They met at an embassy gig and, according to them both, it was nearly love at first sight."

"Nearly?"

"Yeah, well, they gave it a couple of minutes for prudence's sake."

Shannon smiled.

"Anyway, they got married and Dad worked as a junior ambassador for the first five years of their marriage. About that time, my older brother, Mark, came along. Almost immediately after, Dad got posted to the states. A year after the family relocated to D.C., they had me."

"Sounds like you were in line for a fast track to something privileged and prestigious. Why didn't that happen?"

"Temperament, I guess, more than anything. Mom and Dad are very dignified, very traditional, as befits an English ambassador and his distinguished wife. I was afflicted—"

Here, Shannon raised her eyes to his.

"Mom's words. I was afflicted with an unconventional streak right from the cradle. Mom blames it on all the Yank water she drank while she was pregnant."

Shannon leaned back, enjoying his dry delivery.

"Bottom line, politicking and legal protocol have never been my bag. Mark's the conformist of the family."

"How so?"

"He's a high-powered lawyer on Capitol Hill. Me, I prefer a quieter life."

"Yeah. You certainly get that on the force."

Now David smiled and pulled his shake closer to finger his straw. "All right, your turn."

"What do you want to know?" Shannon finished her last fry and contemplated her own malt.

"What is LaCrosse to you?"

Her eyes lifted to David's. The humor she had worn so easily dimmed. "A very good friend. That's all."

"That's all you're going to tell me."

"David, please . . . could we not talk about him tonight? I just want to relax."

"The subject of LaCrosse makes you tense?"

"If you don't stop acting like a cop, I'm going to walk right out that door and hail a cab."

She was serious. David was reminded that he didn't have the right to keep tabs on her life. But then, she'd chosen to be with him tonight when it was obvious that her decision might not make her "friend" too happy.

"So, is the evening ruined?" he ventured.

Shannon seemed to think about it, then looked

beyond him to the laughing diners in the neighboring booth. "No, it's not."

"Then I'd still like to hear about you," he urged, trying to lighten the sudden heaviness between them.

"Well, my story isn't nearly as interesting as yours."

"So tell me anyway."

Shannon pushed her malt aside. "I was born and raised right here in D.C. My family wasn't prestigious—at least, not the foster parents who raised me."

"You were adopted?"

"I was orphaned, then adopted. I became a ward of the state when I was ten. Two years after that, I started getting shuffled around to foster homes until I lucked out on a winner."

"It must have been a good match. You turned out pretty good."

"Yes, well, contrary to popular myth, all foster homes aren't hell holes and all foster parents aren't monsters. The Crosbys were—are—wonderful people."

"I didn't mean to put you on the defensive," David said quietly.

Shannon's expression turned wry. "You didn't, it's me. All through college and still with some of the bureaucracy I run up against now," she shrugged. "I just get tired of sometimes having to defend a system that isn't all bad. It frequently manages to do a pretty fair job. No one could be better living proof of that than me."

"So, the Crosbys," David prompted.

"Miranda and Bob. Great people. They were the first ones to show me that living the street life is not a foregone destiny, based on how and where you were born."

"That explains the social work."

"Probably, yes. I decided early on that I wanted to be there for some other kid who was never going to be as fortunate as I was in getting a great family."

"Laudable."

Shannon shrugged. "I'm not noble."

"You care."

"Yeah, well, judging from your record, so do you."

"Jack again?" David hooked an arm around the back of his seat.

Shannon laughed a bit. "Your partner comes through. With the sincerest affection, I might add."

"Then the question is, why do you care?"

Shannon was slow to answer. "I don't know," she finally said.

David heard the low-voiced conversations and sporadic laughter of the diners around them. He wondered if their conversations were as fraught with undertones as his and Shannon's. "I think I can make a good guess. Will you let me?"

Shannon regarded him seriously.

"I told you once before that I'm attracted to you, Shannon. And you're attracted to me; you've admitted it. So that's one barrier crossed."

"Oh, David, this is unwise," Shannon murmured.

This time, he wanted the full story behind that reluctance; he wanted it on the table between them. "Why does it have to be?" He came away from the back of his bench to lean in close to Shannon. "LaCrosse doesn't have any permanent hold on you. Does he?"

More time passed before Shannon answered, "I'm here with you, aren't I?"

"Shannon, look at me."

She did. As their eyes held, she laid her hand on the table and moved it until her fingers touched his.

David turned his hand over to cushion hers, palm to palm. While he squeezed gently, he murmured, "I'll be right back."

Shannon watched him go. Shortly thereafter, the chattering voices around her were joined by a melodic one. David had punched a dreamy old Motown ballad into the jukebox at the back of the room. When he rejoined her, he didn't sit down. He held out his hand. His mouth curved with an invitation. "Dance?"

Shannon hesitated before she laid her hand in his.

It was hardly the ideal setting for a dance. The aisle was too narrow, the booths beside them too full. And yet they came together with an ease that made other patrons stop their conversations to watch them.

Shannon wound her arms loosely around David's neck. With each slow step they took, they shuffled softly together in place. Shannon leaned into his body, feeling comforted and protected by the strength of his strong hands at her waist.

At her acceptance, David tightened his arms around her. Lazily, he met the eye of an old, grizzled black man sitting two booths down. The man winked. David winked back and inhaled the fragrant warmth of Shannon's closeness. The song was ending when he lowered his mouth to her ear. "Can we go?"

Shannon tensed.

"Honey?"

"Where?" Her answer was as softly rendered as his question.

Another song began. David pulled back and gave her a look. He stepped around her to retrieve his jacket from the booth. When he turned back, she was already heading toward the door.

Outside, David stood close to her, looking down into her eyes. His own were still intense, his voice still soft. "Where do you want to go?"

Shannon lifted a hand to his jaw, letting him make the subtle adjustment that placed his soft kiss against her skin. Her lips parted on a soundless breath before she let her hand drift into a caress against his throat. When his eyes shuttered, snaring her, she let him go. But she didn't back away.

The ride to his home was pensive. But after he parked at the curb, Shannon made no move to get out and David realized she was having second thoughts. He bit down on his disappointment, reminding himself that things were moving fast. "You can change your mind, you know. I'll understand."

Heavy moments ticked by. A car accelerated past them. A child on a bike pedaled furiously by. And then Shannon opened her door.

After a thoughtful moment, David followed.

Inside, moonlight spilled through the massive front room bay window that illuminated the hallway. It led to the foot of a narrow staircase. David took Shannon's hand and tugged, urging her upward. She followed, but at the foot of the first stair she hesitated again.

"What's wrong?" David touched her shoulder.

"What am I doing?" She pulled her hand from his and looked away, running an agitated hand through her hair.

David knew she needed his restraint. But God help him, she'd come this far and he wanted her in his arms. "You're following your heart. What's so terrible about that?"

Shannon didn't bother to hide her quiet tears from him when she looked back up at him. "Two days ago, Peter LaCrosse asked me to marry him. I said yes."

David's stepped away. Just like that, he thought. "What?"

Shannon moved past him. "I'm sorry, David. Coming here . . . making you think . . . I was wrong."

"Then why did you do it?" His disbelief was turning to anger.

Shannon hugged herself, seeming to struggle for an answer. All she said was, "There's nothing I can say to excuse this. I just . . . I just wanted—"

"What? A last good lay before you sold yourself to that old man?"

Shannon flinched.

"Too bad you got cold feet. The way I'm feeling tonight, you would have gotten plenty of what he probably won't or can't give you, despite his inestimable worth."

"David, don't. He doesn't deserve that. Nothing you can say is worse than what I'm telling myself."

Wrong, David thought. If he didn't feel so foolish, he'd laugh at himself for being as blinded by his libido as the rawest teenaged boy. But beyond that, he felt cheated.

Deep down on some level where he'd thought he and Shannon had met tonight, he felt betrayed.

From the front door, Shannon said, "I'll call a cab."

David pulled his keys from his hip pocket. "No, you won't. I'll take you back to your car."

"I really didn't mean to hurt you."

"I'm not the one still making a production of it, Shannon. Let's go."

They didn't speak during the drive back to the precinct. David thought he heard her sniffle once, but in the chilled aftermath of what had almost happened, that consolation seemed very small.

\*   \*   \*

Two months later, she'd married LaCrosse. Two years after that, he laid eyes on her again as she knelt over the body of her dead stepson, crying.

The porch light flicked on. He was discovered. Marshall Baker wondered what he had against Shannon.

Nearly three years of anger. His head warned him that part of her probably really was the cool, calculating enigma who had almost lain in his bed after she'd promised herself to another man.

For that reason alone, he was self-righteously justified in believing she deserved the fate she'd been dealt. And yet . . .

He tossed away the stone in his fist and went inside.

# CHAPTER FIVE

Shannon thought it bizarre and more than a little intimidating to share a first meal with a general population of inmates she'd already served substantial time with. Yet that's exactly the situation in which she found herself one winter morning eighteen months into her sentence.

Her request for release from protective custody had recently been granted, much to the consternation of her lawyer.

But Shannon had persevered because she'd decided if she was going to go crazy having to be locked away, she wasn't going to do it in a state of solitary confinement. Still, the noise and crowd she'd never had the chance to adjust to were making her jittery.

She inched along the breakfast serving line, meeting the frankly curious stares of the other women. Some were more than curious. They were hostile. The unsettled feeling intensified, especially as her eyes collided with those of a heavy-set Latino woman directly in front of her.

Shannon had been trying to ignore the woman,

guessing her game was to get a rise out of the "new" inmate. Now the woman shuffled a couple of steps forward, allowing Shannon to move ahead only fractionally.

A few paces down the line behind them, someone said, "Hey, princess, if you can't do better than this, get out of the way."

"I'm not your problem," Shannon replied and made a show of keeping her attention on the food selection in front of her.

"You ain't' in no fancy restaurant," the woman answered, unwilling to give Shannon the last word. "All we get in here is thirty minutes."

Shannon tensed at the belligerent tone, but she didn't respond. And then the Latino woman made a production of turning around. "You trying to say I'm the problem, girl?"

Shannon swore inwardly. "I wasn't talking to you. I'm just trying to get some breakfast here, like everybody else."

The woman rested her tray against her stomach and leaned a hip against the food rail. "You're lying. You think you're better than everybody in here now, but we know you were raised on the same streets we was." She let her eyes travel slowly over Shannon from head to toe.

The aggression was palpable. Shannon debated what to do. As she'd wanted, she was mingling with this population, and she'd known sooner or later they would test her. That understanding told her now that her only hope of coexisting peacefully was to present a tough face.

It helped to remember the Latino woman had spoken the truth. She *had* grown up on the streets of inner-city D.C. No matter how cushioned her existence had become, there were rules of urban battle she hadn't forgotten.

"Why don't we just keep moving here before we upset the ladies behind us." She was startled at the steel even she heard in her voice.

The Latino woman came away from the rail. "Don't tell me what to do, bitch."

"Hey, hey!" The guard who had been eyeing the exchange from across the room hurried toward the line. "We ain't gonna have no trouble in here this morning, you two. LaCrosse, if you can't keep yourself straight, I'll pull you out of that line myself!"

Shannon swallowed a rush of anger. One glimpse at the amused triumph in her aggressor's eyes, at the matching expressions in several others, cautioned her to bite her tongue. She gripped her tray more tightly and turned back to the food behind the protective glass.

The Latino woman held her ground a little longer before she finally turned away, too. The line started moving again.

Shannon's heart was still racing as she assembled an unexciting selection of grits, rubbery sausage, and watery baked apples. She spotted an empty table beneath one of the room's few meshed windows and headed that way.

She'd just taken her seat when an inmate she hadn't noticed helped herself to the opposite chair.

This woman appeared to be a few years older than she was, maybe mid-thirties. Her hair was neatly gathered into a bun at her nape.

Fine lines of dissipation marred features that, Shannon guessed, had been strikingly pretty before drugs or alcohol, or whatever vice she had indulged in, had taken a toll.

"My name's Rose," the woman said. "I know who you are."

"Who doesn't?"

The woman gave Shannon a quick, assessing look. "We heard you were coming, but they locked you away awful fast." She bit into the dry toast she picked up from her sparsely filled plate. "Was that your doing or theirs?"

"Theirs." Shannon wasn't going to elaborate to a stranger, no matter how cordial the inquiry seemed.

"That's what I heard."

Shannon glanced up sharply, but since Rose wasn't forthcoming, she started in on her own meal.

"So, you really killed your husband's kid, huh?"

Shannon forced down her next bite. "It was an accident."

Rose laughed. "Yeah, honey, that's what manslaughter is. An accident."

"That's not what I meant."

Rose eyed Shannon while she picked up her napkin and dabbed at the corner of her mouth. "I know what you're saying."

Feeling oddly compelled not to leave it alone, Shannon continued, "The press had it all wrong. Jeff wasn't my lover."

"You're saying you're innocent."

"Yes."

Rose turned back to her meal. "Well, that's too bad, then. But I'll tell you something. You ain't the first innocent to get locked up in here. It's for damn sure you ain't gonna be the last."

Shannon studied the rest of her food, but couldn't finish it. She pushed away her tray. "Why are you in here?"

"Murder." Rose's head came up. "And guess what? I ain't innocent."

That gave Shannon pause, as she was sure it was meant to do.

Rose shrugged, already dismissing it. "He deserved it, the crazy son of a bitch. But I didn't sit down here to talk about me."

"Then what do you want?"

"To warn you. Watch out for Jodie." Rose nodded to their right.

Shannon looked two tables down and saw the woman who had tried to pick the fight with her in line. She was laughing in response to something one of her tablemates was saying. Then as if she sensed the extra attention, her brooding gaze found and locked onto Shannon.

Shannon looked away. "What does she want?"

Rose laughed. "Honey, even Daphne over there—" She pointed at a slight black woman hunched over her plate at the adjoining table.

"—ain't that naive. What do you *think* she wants?"

Pensive, Shannon let her gaze touch and linger on Daphne. The woman raised her eyes only to dart quick glances around her. Shannon was reminded of something sad and mistreated.

"Now, the thing to do," Rose was saying, "is to be *smart*. You listen to me. A woman's got to use her head to survive in here. And sometimes that survival means concentrating on a lot more than how slow time's crawling by."

Rose pushed her tray aside and laid down her napkin. "You know what I mean?" she murmured, watching Shannon closely.

Shannon's attention drifted back to Rose.

"Hm, honey? Do you?"

Suddenly Shannon did and was chilled. She was seeking a strategic response when Rose smiled again. Quite audibly, she said, "Jodie ain't nothing but a big bully. Don't you let her push you around." And then she reached out to stroke Shannon's jaw. "Everybody in here ain't her friend." With a lingering look, she picked up her tray and sauntered away.

Shannon had thought she'd been prepared for anything from these women. But Jodie's aggressiveness and now Rose's subtleties only left her feeling embarrassed and confused.

Abruptly, it occurred to her to wonder who else had taken in her conversation. A quick glance around revealed the answer. Several pairs of eyes were locked onto her. Some seemed to wonder what she would do. Others only looked amused.

Jodie didn't look amused. In fact, if anything, her attention intensified.

"Jesus," Shannon thought, knowing she wouldn't do herself any good to panic. Her immediate challenge was to figure out how to survive.

The space was adequate, David judged, even if it was only one half of the double he was going to finish renovating and move into after he resigned from the force.

He backed down the ladder from where he'd been touching up some drywall, notched down the radio at his feet, and sauntered over to a worktable to open the cooler of beer he'd brought from home. He reached for a can now, thinking about his decision to open his own private investigation agency.

Very shortly, any professional headaches or petty irritations he encountered would be strictly of his own making. They wouldn't be byproducts of bureaucratic administrators who worried about covering their own asses more than they did about upholding the spirit of the law when that spirit conflicted with expediency.

He sipped his beer and allowed his mind to wander to Shannon and the LaCrosse shooting. Perhaps the aftermath and a little jump-starting from Marshall Baker had given him the final push he'd needed to act on his decision to leave the force. God knew he'd been toying with a personal and professional restlessness that had caused him to procrastinate on making the decision for more than a year.

But Baker and plain common sense had helped remind him of what he already knew deep down: a restless cop was a dangerous cop, if not a dead one. And thoughts of restlessness led him back to Shannon and Jeffrey LaCrosse.

The few leads in the case that had existed originally after the shooting were so cold now he'd had to take special measures to generate a spark. So far, the spark hadn't kindled, and he was thinking he needed to update Baker when someone knocked on the double doors that opened out onto the street.

David set his beer down and went to open it. Jack peered at him through the newly installed beveled window. David opened up. "Hey, man, I can use the help." He let Jack in. "Tools are on the table; I'll show you where to start."

Jack closed the door behind him. "Actually, I came to talk."

His hammer in hand, David reached the foot of the ladder and kept his back to his partner. "What about?"

"You."

David climbed a couple of steps and positioned a nail against the section of wall he'd been securing. "Nothing particular's going on with me." He started hammering.

"I think this is important."

David fished another nail out of his utility apron. "Sounds like it."

"Somebody's tossing money around on the street. Something to do with Shannon LaCrosse."

"And?"

"You know about it?"

David turned. "How do you?"

"I was taking a walk around my old neighborhood, mainly to browse around that store Maria likes. Jim, the owner, starts telling me he's just hired this kid named Tonio Clyde, new to the city.

"Jim calls Clyde over to tell him he'd better be good to me because I'm a cop and the place needs all the protection it can get." Jack walked over to an outer window to watch a car cruise down the street.

David waited.

"So the next thing I know, the kid comes up to me when I'm alone down one of the aisles. He says Jim told him I'm partnered with a cop named Courtney and that he's got some information Courtney wants. He says there's talk that Shannon LaCrosse may have found herself a sweetie on the inside and that the buzz has really pissed off one of his new friends."

"Who's the friend?"

"Punk. Jerard Booley."

David grunted. "I know him. I busted him a few months back for possession. What was he pissed off for?"

"Tonio says they were drinking some and Booley started going on about how he should have made it with Shannon himself when he had the chance, before her dyke got her."

David turned back to the wall, alert. This was something. "The kid tell you anything else?"

"That I owed him. My little run to the deli turned into one damned expensive trip, man." Jack held out his hand. "You owe me. He told me how much. And why are you throwing around that kind of money anyway?"

David reached for his wallet, pulled out some cash, laid it in Jack's hand.

"All right, let me restate that. What are you playing around with? The LaCrosse case is history. You're not doing something you're going to wind up regretting—career-wise, I mean?"

David finished with the wall and came down off the ladder. He reached for his beer. "Look around you. I'm taking charge of my career."

"Yeah. Well, just remember something. As far as I'm concerned, this partner thing has a statute of limitations that extends beyond the job."

David smiled. "I know. If what I need comes out of this, I'll tell you about it."

Tonio Clyde never suspected the drunk who bumped into him was stone-cold sober. But Markey Shaw's concentration couldn't have been clearer. He watched Clyde swing inside a hamburger joint, then he slid inside a corner phone booth a few feet away to dial the beeper number he'd been given.

His contact rang him back less than a minute

later and Shaw picked up. "I followed Courtney's partner inside a grocery here. The kid I told you about gave him some information. Sounded like it was about Booley and Shannon LaCrosse."

"Does David Courtney know you?"

"No."

"Then focus exclusively on him, on whoever else takes his money. Keep me informed and I'll keep paying you."

Shaw hung up.

On the other side of town, inside a five-star hotel, another man replaced the phone receiver on a wall near a ballroom door. He nodded at a passing waiter who hustled a tray of champagne back inside to the local celebrity crowd.

The man idly watched the waiter's moves, reflecting on Peter's decision to push on reopening Shannon's case. He appeared calm. His calculating thoughts were anything but.

"Hello, Peter." Shannon stood before her husband with no barrier between them this time. The absence of it was another casualty of protective custody whose loss she wasn't always sure she appreciated.

Peter looked wary. Shannon wondered if he would claim the first of their two permissible hugs. He did, but with disheartening hesitation.

Just as tentatively, she returned it. This was the first time in nearly two years she'd felt her husband's embrace. She thought it sad that her overwhelming awareness was only of the guard's intrusive eyes.

Peter let her go and backed away to his chair. Shannon stepped back to hers. The gray walls of the visitation area absorbed their silence as dispassionately as she and her husband absorbed the murmured conversations around them.

"How are you, Shannon?"

"It's been a long time, Peter. Again."

"I didn't mean to stay away so long."

"Then why did you?"

"My last visit upset you."

"Are you surprised?" Shannon's smile was sardonic.

Peter stared down at his folded hands. "We both needed some time to reevaluate." He looked back up at her. "I needed some time."

With that glimmer of frankness, Shannon started to relax. "I can't change the past. I loved you."

Peter smiled sadly. "Loved? Past tense?"

"So much has happened, Peter." She sighed heavily. "Of course I still have feelings for you."

"But not love?"

"Please, don't push."

Peter looked away.

So did Shannon, hating this awkwardness, hating the fact that they couldn't get beyond it. She searched for something mundane. "How's the business?"

"Good." Peter rubbed the back of his neck.

He's lying, Shannon thought, surprised. Ever

since she'd known him, he'd been energized by just the thought of his company. Now he just looked stressed. And ill.

"How good?" she pressed, with genuine curiosity.

"Hectic just now. Alan and I are working on a particularly sensitive deal."

"That concerns?"

Peter hesitated. "It's too premature to talk about."

Shannon frowned. "It never used to be, not with me."

"I know."

"Tell me, Peter, please. I'd like to believe we're at least still friends."

He started to say something then changed his mind. "No. I didn't come here to burden you with my problems."

"Problems?"

"Shannon—"

"All right." She backed off, seeing that he wasn't willing to give her more just now. "Tell me what else is going on."

Peter leaned forward. "What I really came here to talk to you about is something Marshall's working on. It could get you out of here."

Shannon stared at him startled, afraid to hope. "Are you serious?"

Peter nodded. "He may have located the man you say harassed you."

"How?" Shannon wondered what detail could

have revealed itself now, nearly two years after the fact.

"He's been aided by someone neither of us was too sure we could trust. David Courtney. I guess he finally remembered he used to be your friend."

"David is helping me?" Shannon repeated.

"Yes. Ironic, isn't it?"

Shannon leaned back. He had no idea.

# CHAPTER SIX

David was tired and irritable, and wanted nothing more than to go home. Jerard Booley didn't seem to share his sentiment, judging by how long he'd been inside the building he'd entered several cold hours ago.

A streetlight diffused minimal light across the front of the lot David had parked in. He tilted his watch toward the bit of light that filtered inside the car. It was going on one a.m. His shift started in six hours. He hadn't been home in sixteen.

"Come on, Booley, come out of there." He shifted again, seeking whatever comfort he could for a cold butt that had already gone numb.

He'd been running his last conversation with Jack in his head all day. Why had Booley's name been the one to surface? Not because of coincidence, he'd bet. That's why he'd tapped sources about Booley's probable whereabouts, which had put him here.

He was glaring at the heater he couldn't turn on when the front door of the building opened. Three men walked out. Booley was one of them.

David watched all three hunch against the icy drizzle that began to fall. Booley turned his coat collar up and headed north. The other two headed south.

Good, David thought, starting his car to follow Booley.

At the corner, he caught up and tapped his horn. Booley didn't break stride, but he looked around to investigate. David saw recognition hit him, along with an understanding that he wouldn't get far if he ran.

David pulled up even with Booley, then reached over to throw open the passenger door. "Get in."

"Ah, man, what you smokin' me out for?" But Booley threw himself inside.

"I want to talk. Relax, you'll get coffee for it."

"For what?"

"Whatever you know about Shannon LaCrosse."

Booley shook his head and muttered, "Shit."

David drove two streets over. "What's the deal, Jerard?" He pulled into a convenience store lot, ordered, "Stay put," then palmed his keys and got out.

From inside the store, he watched Booley through the window. Booley pushed open his door, considered getting out, then yanked himself back inside.

David smiled and paid for their coffees. Back outside in the cold, cups in hand, he gestured at Booley through the passenger window. Booley lowered it and David handed a styrofoam cup in to him through the gap. Back behind the wheel, he stored his own cup in the beverage holder under the dash, then put the car into gear.

The back of the lot looked fairly deserted and David headed there, cutting the engine. He sipped and waited. Out of the corner of his eye, he saw Booley's hands tremble as he raised his cup.

"All right," David prompted. "I said tell me what you know."

"I know lots of things, but you wanted to talk about Shannon LaCrosse. Okay. She's a juicy little piece. Always was, even when we was kids. I tried to get me some then, but she wouldn't give it up 'cause she was already a snooty bitch."

"Cut the bullshit," David commented.

Booley finished his coffee, crushed his empty cup, and dropped it on the floor between his feet.

"Let's try again." idly, David began to tap the steering wheel.

"What did Shannon tell you?" Booley hedged.

"We're here to talk about what *you're* going to tell me. You've already admitted that's something." David set his own empty cup back inside the holder. "So tell me."

"Or what?"

"Or I'm going to seriously harass your ass, Jerard," he said harshly. "You know I can."

Booley sighed, frustrated. "Okay. I made some phone calls to her once a long time ago."

Damn, David thought. "Why?"

Booley laughed, a nasty sound. "To tell her what a pretty little brown ass she had."

"I didn't pull you in to listen to your wet dreams, asshole. Give me substance."

"Fuck you, Courtney. I told her what I was ordered to."

"Who gave the orders?"

"I don't know."

That made David turn to him. "What do you mean you don't know?"

"A guy I know approaches me one day to tell me I can make money. All I have to do is what he tells me to. I got two hundred up front."

"Details, Jerard."

"I was supposed to scare Shannon."

"And?"

"And make her think she was going to die."

David started the car. "You're coming down to the station tomorrow morning. You're going to repeat what you've just said, plus a lot more, only this time you're going to do it on tape with witnesses."

"Ah, man, I don't wanna—"

"What did I tell you! I know about the chemicals you and your buddies were playing with inside that house tonight. I'll roust you all. That means you in particular. Now and the next time and the next, because I'm going to stay on you until you realize you've got no place to go."

Sullen, Booley glared straight ahead.

David swung the car out onto the dark two-laned road. "So what's it going to be, Jerard?"

"Fuck you, Courtney."

David smiled.

"Sir, I'm leaving for the night. There's coffee on in the kitchen if you still want some."

"Excellent, Helen, thanks. See you in the morning." The Iceman watched his secretary pull his door closed behind her. Before it clicked completely shut, his mind was already considering what had been preoccupying him when she'd interrupted.

Peter was as firmly in the spell of his wife as he'd been the day they'd put her in jail. *Dammit.* Well, he couldn't be convinced . . . so there was no choice.

Jeff had been an unplanned but ultimately necessary means to an end. Who would have thought that that vital part of Peter's spirit he'd prized so highly would die right along with his son? Furthermore, his passion for the business, which had faltered after Jeff's death, had all but flickered out with Shannon's imprisonment. Peter was now an obstruction and had to be moved out of the way.

Arnaud and the other Worldcom powerbrokers weren't prepared to wait, and neither was he.

He turned to the credenza behind him, picked up his phone, and dialed.

\*    \*    \*

The next morning at the station after he had brought the attending officers up to speed, David told Booley, "All right, from the top."

Jerard Booley cleared his throat and stared at the condensation-soaked can of soda sitting in front of him. "My name is Jerard Booley . . ." He gave his occupation (unemployed) and his address (his mother's), then glanced over at David, who watched him across the room from his perch on the windowsill.

"Tell us about your conversations with Shannon," David prompted. "And be specific."

"I did that two years ago, over—" He sucked in his lips. "—two months or so, off and on."

David gauged the impassive looks of the other officers. He detected a bit more interest, and then dawning understanding, from Jack. "Who approached you?" He urged Booley, looking back at him.

"Dude named Markey. Markey Shaw."

David couldn't place the name. He caught Jack's eye again. Jack nodded and left the room. David turned back to Booley. "Do you know why?"

"Why what?"

"Why the threats, genius?" another detective piped up.

Booley shrugged. "I didn't care. I just wanted the money. Markey told me to make the threats sound real, and I guess I did. She eventually plugged her old man's kid, didn't she?"

David just looked at him.

Booley dropped his eyes.

"So what happened before that?" David asked.

"So I eventually told Markey that Shannon sounded like she really was starting to panic, almost like she thought she had nowhere to turn."

"What did Markey do?"

"He told me my part was nearly finished."

David thought about that. He'd follow it up later. "Did you ever tell Shannon LaCrosse outright that you were going to kill her?"

Booley wrapped his hands around his soda can.

David could feel him weighing the strength of the noose around his neck, figuring the minimum he could get away with revealing before the rope tightened completely.

Booley finally answered, "I told her if she didn't leave LaCrosse, she was dead."

"That wasn't my question, Jerard. I said, did you ever tell Shannon over the phone outright that *you* personally were going to come to her house to kill her?"

Booley took a drink, swallowed too fast, coughed a little. "Maybe," he muttered. "Once."

"What? Speak up, you're fading out of the tape."

Booley slammed his soda down on the table. "I said I did it once! Like I was told."

David left the sill. He straddled a chair beside Booley and folded his hands. "When you told her that, did you say when? When you were coming for her?"

"No. And you can't nail me down that tight

because I didn't know what night it was set for!''

What *night* it was set for? Maybe not, Booley, but you knew more about what was planned to go down than you're saying here right now, David thought. And that's less than I'm going to get out of you later.

David ran a hand around the back of his neck, feeling the weight of guilt and wasted time that had passed on Shannon's behalf.

Another detective said, ''Jerard, we're going to run this tape you've just made against some others, to compare . . .''

David half-listened. After Booley was taken back into custody, he headed for his office. He owed Baker a call.

Shannon never heard Jodie come up behind her. One moment she was untying her robe, the next she was being shoved into the tiny shower stall in front of her. Jodie turned the spray on hard, soaking the robe and the cotton gown beneath, and muffling her cry against her hand.

''Rosie ain't around to look out after you now, bitch, is she!'' Jodie snaked her other hand under Shannon's gown, clamping it brutally on the front of her thigh.

Shannon jerked violently, sensing the other woman's need to hurt. She forced herself to take slow breaths against the suffocating cushion of Jodie's hand.

''What you got to say, now, Miss High and

Mighty?" Jodie laughed, then her voice turned mean. "Nothing, that's what, 'cause I got you just where I want you." She moved in closer behind Shannon until she crowded her back.

The water pounded down on Shannon, pounded around her. The white tile wall filled her vision. Now or never, she told herself.

She jerked her head back sharply into Jodie's chin, throwing the woman off balance, creating the opening she needed. While Jodie stumbled, Shannon bit down hard into the soft, pudgy flesh of Jodie's hand.

Jodie yelped and staggered, but she didn't buckle this time. Still, Shannon shoved past her.

She lurched to the shallow shelf above the sink and snatched her towel, groping inside for the weapon she and Rose had devised.

Jodie was turning around, her face red with anger, to charge Shannon—when she stumbled to a stop. The slightest move would have driven the tip of Shannon's makeshift knife into the soft folds of her throat.

Shannon was shaking, but not too much to take a firmer grip on the shank in her hand. She'd never been so grateful for listening to Rose as when the older woman had advised her how an ordinary ink pen could be fitted for her protection with a concealed blade.

She jabbed now at Jodie's throat and made enough contact to draw a tiny fleck of blood. "If you ever touch me again, *ever*, I swear to God I'll hurt you. The same goes for your friends." Jodie shrank back. "You tell them that. *Tell* them!"

"Hey, what's going on in there?" The loud question startled Shannon and pushed her a step back from Jodie. She curled her fist around the knife, hiding it, just as a guard rushed onto the scene. Jodie, still stunned and furious, stared at Shannon. The guard looked from one to the other then settled on Shannon.

"Get out of here, LaCrosse. You ain't been nothing but trouble since they took you out of custody. Go on!" she ordered.

Shannon stood her ground long enough to reinforce what she'd told Jodie. She was sickened by the intensity of rage she felt—and grateful for the feeling of empowerment it gave her.

Still trembling, she gathered her towel and squeezed past the guard, who continued to glare at her.

In the hallway, a handful of women had gathered. Rose was standing slightly apart from them. Before she and the others dispersed, she gave Shannon a very faint smile.

Later at dinner, Shannon was surprised when another inmate accompanied Rose to the table. Rose introduced the mousy little woman Shannon remembered having seen once before.

"Daphne Collins, meet Shannon LaCrosse."

Daphne mumbled, "Hi," and sat down.

"Hi," Shannon uttered back, looking over the woman's head at Rose. Rose simply shrugged.

Then Daphne made an effort to speak again. She laid down her fork and looked Shannon in the eye. "I heard about this morning, about you telling Jodie to go to hell. Is it true?"

"Yes," Shannon answered slowly as Daphne paused over a bite of her food. Then the little woman smiled.

Again, Shannon met Rose's eyes.

Rose winked, daintily picked at her own food, and said, "Daphne ain't the only one who's taken notice."

Shannon stared at her for a moment. "I don't know what to say to that. I'm not proud of what I've done." The necessity for it still felt unreal to her. Rose seemed to read her mind.

"You won't be having no more trouble any time soon out of Jodie. You did more than preserve your virtue today, little girl. You earned yourself some serious respect."

"By threatening to kill a woman?"

"By demonstrating you'll do what it takes to protect yourself, to save your life. If you want that lesson to stick, you'd better not start backing away from it now."

"That's right," Daphne said. "Your life in here won't be worth shit if you do."

Shannon looked at Daphne. Daphne looked solemnly back. Shannon understood, shaking her head. "I just never actually thought I'd have to do something like that."

Rose said, "Well, it's done and Jodie won't forget it."

The three women finished eating in silence, each guarding her own thoughts. Daphne was the first to leave the table. Shannon took a long drink from her water glass while she watched the woman go.

"Shannon."

Shannon set the glass down and looked at Rose. "What?"

"I think the time has come for you to understand something else now, something I want to have plain between us."

Rose's quiet gravity made Shannon tense all over again. "Okay," she said warily.

"When you first came out into the population, when I started showing you the ropes, I didn't make too many bones about what I wanted from you in return."

Shannon dropped her eyes to her napkin. "I know," she murmured uncomfortably. "I've always been grateful for your settling for the pretense, our public appearance of intimacy, because it's given me the protection I've needed to get by."

Rose nodded. "You also know how I didn't ask for more than that public hand holding and hugging because I know you ain't about that. When you treated me decent, I figured that was something I had to respect. Today you've proven you can fend for yourself, that you're worthy of my respect. That's why out of respect I'm going to shoot straight with you now."

"Meaning?"

"Meaning the time might come when I ask you again."

Shannon was still staring at Rose when the other woman picked up her tray and left the table.

# CHAPTER SEVEN

"Shannon, what's wrong?" Marshall gripped her hand, his concession to the permissible hug. When she didn't answer, he let go, sat down, and said, "I've got some great news."

"Well, your timing couldn't be better." She gazed out at the other inmates and visitors around them.

Marshall was alarmed. "Are you all right?"

"I'm surviving in here, Marshall. It's just that the price for doing it can be pretty damned high."

Marshall looked at Shannon more carefully. She had always been slender. Now she was starting to look gaunt. The circles under her eyes were pronounced. "Have you been eating?"

Shannon laughed bitterly. "This isn't the sort of place that encourages an appetite."

Marshall noted her calmness. He wasn't at all convinced she was for real. "Hopefully that isn't something you'll have to worry about much longer."

"Tell me," Shannon said.

"We tracked down—or rather I should say,

Courtney tracked down—the man who harassed you. He's also admitted to threatening your life.''

Shannon wanted to feel overjoyed, but Marshall's news seemed depressingly distant from her greater concern—preserving her emotional stability, if not her life. "What happens now?"

"You're not taking this like I thought you would," Marshall said, frowning.

"Answer the question."

Marshall watched her a minute longer, still frowning. "What happens is, I petition the court for another hearing. With this new evidence, we argue again that you acted in self-defense. If we can convince the court of that, your conviction gets overturned and you're out of here."

"How long?"

"I'm sorry?"

"How long for all of this to happen?"

"I'm filing the paperwork this afternoon. I'm hoping we can actually get it to court in a month, no more than two."

Shannon looked away. "That long."

"Shannon, dammit, what's wrong?"

At length, she said, "I think I've sold my soul to the devil."

"You've been threatened, haven't you? Dammit, I told you leaving protective custody was wrong. I'm getting you back in."

"No."

"What?"

"I said, no. I mean it." And Shannon realized she really did.

It was an odd thing, but for most of her life the fear of one thing or another had dictated her acquiescence in too many things. The latest example of that, of maneuvering herself into a position of weakness in here by trusting someone else's strength instead of her own, nurtured a new need.

For better or worse, she had to prove to herself that she was strong enough this time to deal with the consequences of her actions.

Her bid for security, for Peter's protection as his wife, may have put her in line for her current fate. That she'd truly loved him in spite of her neediness didn't matter.

The fact was, Rose's ultimatum demonstrated clearly that she was going to have to fight for her survival. And that meant starting by proving to herself that she could.

"You do what you have to do, legally, Marshall. I'll take care of myself in here."

"If you think I'm going to meekly accept that, you're crazy."

Shannon leaned forward. "Listen to me. *Listen.* This is *my* life. More than anything in this world, I want out of here. But if I can't have that I won't live in fear. If that means I have to play as roughly as the other women, I will. So do your job, Marshall. But other than that, butt out."

Baker felt sobered by the iron in Shannon's resolution. "You just hang on, then, just hang on and watch yourself. And swear you'll get in touch if things in here deteriorate."

Shannon stood up. "Good-bye, Marshall." She let the guard escort her out.

"Shannon?"

Shannon opened her eyes and saw Rose standing above her where she sat alone, against the exercise yard wall. "What do you want?"

"I'm asking."

Shannon took a deep breath. She noted the other inmates pausing here and there in their conversations to see what she would do. She looked back at Rose. "No."

Rose's eyes flickered.

Shannon saw regret before that fragile emotion dissolved into something still and resolute. Rose turned from her and walked away.

"Peter, we've got it." Baker straightened some papers on his desk while he balanced the phone between his shoulder and ear. "Proctor and his prosecution team are poised to cave in under the weight of what we've turned up through Booley. The evidence is compelling enough that they can't deny it warrants a new trial. That news leads to this—the court has agreed to hear Shannon's case three weeks from now."

"Three weeks? Is that the best you can do?" LaCrosse rubbed a hand over his chest and pulled open his desk drawer. He took out a bottle of pills recently prescribed to him.

"Yes, and believe me, I pushed. It's not bad. In fact, I don't think I'm being premature to say that

I probably can get Proctor to drop his opposition altogether. But—'' The papers stilled. "What's happening to Shannon, Peter? You're seeing her regularly. I can't get her to tell me what's going on."

"I wish to God I knew. She's not talking to me, either." Reluctantly, LaCrosse added, "I don't think she trusts me."

Marshall huffed. "You're crazy. The woman loves you."

"Yes, before Jeff's death. Now . . . But I love *her*."

"Then you have to hold on to that, Peter. Time is on your side and hers."


"Shannon, compliments of Rosie."

The attack came hard and fast. One minute, Shannon was walking into the exercise yard, the next her arms were being restrained by two women while four others clustered in front of them, shielding what was going on.

Shannon tried to shout, to attract attention, but couldn't. The first blow drove into her stomach, forcing her down. After that, the hits stayed punishing. Once, she tried to pull her arms free to protect her face. It was useless.

The lesson had been ordained and was being carried out with a brutality Shannon would take months to forget.

Then as suddenly as it began, the beating stopped. Shannon lay on the ground in too much pain to move. Dimly, she saw the guard who had been conveniently out of sight approaching.

"Get out of the way, out of the way!" the woman ordered the crowding inmates. Then everything in Shannon's vision faded until she heard no more.

"Courtney."

"Yeah, you caught me on my way out, Baker."

"For this, you'll want to slow down."

Shannon, David thought. He pulled his desk chair back around.

"Shannon was attacked in the prison yard yesterday."

"*Goddammit*, I knew something like this was going to happen." David felt shaken. The guilt that had ridden him since Jerard Booley's confession intensified. He tightened his hand on the telephone receiver. "How bad?"

"She's alive. They beat her to hell, but they could have done worse. The attending guard claims she didn't see a thing until too late."

Right, David thought. "Where's Shannon now?"

"Prison hospital. Miraculously nothing's broken but she's going to have some damn nasty bruises. I got a court order to move her back into protective custody until the new hearing."

"What about the women who assaulted her?"

Marshall sighed. "Nobody saw anything, so there's no one to be disciplined. Just another unfortunate accident in the routine of prison life."

David rubbed his temple. "You sure nobody can get to her?"

"Nobody will. I pulled strings, got some police protection for her independent of the prison. As long as she's there, she's safe."

"Can you get the trial date moved up?

"I'm sure as hell going to try."

"Shannon, can you hear me?"

Shannon heard Peter's voice, but it was wrong. He sounded very far away, as if what he was saying was being filtered through a tunnel. Then she felt his hand envelop hers. She opened her eyes.

Peter looked hazy until that haze around his face gradually cleared. Suddenly, Shannon remembered and tried to lift her free hand to her own face.

"It's bandaged," Peter soothed, watching her slender fingers go to one eye.

"The doctors say it'll heal," Betty Morris ventured timidly, stepping into Shannon's sight.

Shannon felt a rush of unwelcome surprise to see her sister-in-law. She bitterly resented the woman and the presumption that had brought her here. The last thing she wanted from Betty was some cloying overture of friendship after she had so deeply wronged her.

Then she looked back at her husband and felt the rage of what had been done to her rush back to overwhelm her. "I felt so helpless, Peter. There was nothing I could do to stop them. Nothing."

"I know, baby, but you survived. You're alive and soon you're going to be free."

Shannon pulled her hand from his and turned to the wall.

"Shannon, did you hear me?"

"Yes," she answered listlessly. The problem was, she couldn't comprehend why that should matter. Their marriage was in tatters and so was her life. Peter claimed to love her; she knew he felt sorry for her. But he'd never been able to believe her about Jeff. So where did that leave them?

And then there was that most pressing question of all. Recently, it had begun to constantly plague her. Why was she *really* in here?

She had been set up to shoot Jeff. It seemed the only real explanation for the phone calls and intimidation that had driven her to the shooting and this incarceration. In fact, but for a twist of fate, the caller, Jerard Booley, would never have been found.

Why? *Why?*

"Did you hear me, Shannon?"

She turned back to Peter. "What?"

"I said you're going to be all right. I've set up a trust fund that will keep you comfortable for the rest of your life."

"A trust fund? I don't want your money, Peter. I never did." She'd wanted his faith. She turned back to the wall.

"I know that, Shannon." Peter's sigh was soul deep. "Whatever has become of us now, it's important to me that you believe that."

And what about me, she thought? What about what I wanted you to believe of me? She could hear herself pleading for the same measure of understanding from Peter. How ironic. And tragic. "Keep your guilt money, Peter; I don't want it."

Peter groped inside his suit coat pocket for his pills.

Shannon was startled to see him do it. "What are those?"

LaCrosse twisted off the lid and shook out two pills. He dry-swallowed them. "For my heart." He closed his eyes while the palpitation passed.

His heart? Shannon took a really good look at him. Again, she noted his haggard appearance and, beneath that, a frightening pallor. "You've never had heart trouble before." She looked questioningly at Betty, who looked at her brother. At the cautioning shake of his head, Betty gazed down at her purse in her lap.

Peter got up to close the door. Back at Shannon's bedside, he said, "I've been experiencing small episodes lately. The doctor says it's job stress. Whatever it is, I've got it under control."

"*Job* stress? You love the business."

"Yes."

"Then—?"

"Betty, would you mind waiting outside for me?"

Betty looked a little startled, as if she were pulling her thoughts back from somewhere distant. "Of course. You two need some time." She hesitated before reaching around Peter to touch Shannon's hand that lay against the spread. "We'll talk again soon. If you can just forgive me—"

"Betty," Peter urged.

"Okay. I'll just be outside."

Peter watched Shannon's face while his sister left the room. When the door clicked behind her, he said, "Alan has been pushing for a financial diversification I'm not comfortable with."

"So? You're the senior partner."

"That's always been to my advantage, yes. But for some reason he won't listen to me now. I'm starting to hear rumblings from the board as well."

"Peter—" But seeing that he was anticipating another attack from her on his brother, Shannon switched to a different track. "What's the diversification about?"

"Commercial ventures into properties I don't view as lucrative. Alan insists our corporate eggs have lain in the same baskets for too long, that spreading out our commercial interests is imperative for the company to stay competitive."

"Yes, that always was Alan's tune."

"Dammit, don't start! I know you've never liked him, but this isn't about your differences. This is purely business."

"Peter, I—"

"I know what you think about him, Shannon. But the truth is, if it weren't for Alan playing mediator, I wouldn't have the strained rapport with my board that I'm barely holding onto now."

Shannon took a mental breath. She'd always

had to fight this stubborn allegiance to his brother. And now it suddenly seemed even harder to do because of the physical toll Peter's struggle was so dramatically taking on him. "Just stay alert, that was all I was going to say. Watch what Alan says, what he does."

Peter stood up abruptly. "You need to get some rest, and I've got a meeting in—" He looked at his watch "—thirty minutes."

Shannon watched him turn for the door, looking for the first time since she'd known him like an old man. "Peter?"

LaCrosse didn't turn around.

"Take care of yourself. Please."

Peter looked over his shoulder and smiled sadly. "No matter what you believe, Shannon, I do love you. I always have and I always will."

Shannon watched him go, never suspecting that she would never see him alive again.

Two weeks later Shannon left the hospital. One week after that, she was back in court listening to Jerard Booley's taped threats for the first time since the first trial. Booley corroborated on the stand all that he'd confessed to the police. Baker's supporting argument for Shannon's original assertions of self-defense followed.

And two days later, the verdict Shannon hadn't dared hope would really happen was granted. Her conviction was overturned. She was free.

For the second time, she sat stunned in a courtroom while her judge left the bench. Then Marshall turned to her and leaned down to pull her up from her seat into his jubilant embrace. She returned the gesture a little less heartily.

The vindication she felt was long overdue. Still, her victory felt hollow.

Peter had conveyed his wish for luck through Marshall, because in the end he'd chosen to await the verdict at home. That sustained ambivalence about her, despite the championing role he'd played in seeking her freedom, depressed her.

"Shannon, smile," Marshall coaxed softly. That he understood her emotions was clear in his somber eyes. "Peter will come around. I've known him for a long time and I've yet to know him to be an unfair man. It's this grief that's driving him."

"It's been almost two years, Marshall. How long does the worst of anyone's grief last?"

Marshall squeezed her hand. "Listen, tonight we're going to concentrate on *your* future. There's no sadness allowed. My wife and I are taking you out to dinner."

"I don't know."

"We won't let you say no."

But in the end, no one went. At seven o'clock that evening, Marshall received word that his client and longtime friend Peter LaCrosse had died from a heart attack in his sleep. Long afterward, he would remember the hollow silence of Shannon's reaction when he phoned to tell her that her husband was dead.

\*    \*    \*

David looked at the wall clock over the water cooler. Nine o'clock. He snapped off his desk lamp, throwing his cubicle into a pool of shadows in the after-hours squad room.

He slid some papers from the case file he'd been working on back inside their folder and thought of how he'd stood inside the courtroom earlier. Just long enough to hear the verdict. He'd been relieved for Shannon's sake, but he'd still walked away.

He had no illusions. No matter how pleased she was bound to be, he wouldn't be among her desired well-wishers. His reticence two years ago to push for a harder look into her allegations, no matter how professionally justified he'd felt, had helped send her to prison.

And now to complicate matters, Marshall Baker had just called to tell him Peter LaCrosse was dead.

Dammit. Shannon should have been celebrating today. Instead, here was another curve fate had thrown to mess with her life.

For his own part, he'd taken a first step toward making it up to her for letting his personal grudge overrule the professional aggression he knew he should have exercised to help keep her out of jail in the first place. He was going to delve deeper into Booley. And he wasn't going to let it rest there. The mystery behind the LaCrosse shooting wouldn't be over this time until he was personally satisfied with the answers.

He'd start by looking more closely at this Markey Shaw. That meant he needed to get more information out of Jerard Booley.

"David, you still here?"

David looked up to see Jack walking over to him. "I thought you were gone."

"I'm just leaving." Jack stood in front of David's desk. "The check I ran on this Markey Shaw turned up nothing in the records. We're still looking, but—you think Booley was being straight about the name?"

David shrugged. "Why lie? He's already in deep enough shit on this thing to want to spread around the stink. I've got some sources. Maybe they know something the cops don't." He noted Jack's concerned expression. "What?"

"Didn't you hear?"

David nodded, reminded again. "Yeah, it's another bad break for Shannon." He stood up and bent from the waist, relieving the kinks.

"I'd have thought she'd been cheering."

David gave Jack a sharp look. "That's a little callous, friend. She was having her problems with LaCrosse, but I doubt she wanted to see him dead."

"LaCrosse? What are you talking about?"

David cocked his head. "What are you?"

"Jerard Booley. They found him with a needle up his arm in his cell. It still had traces of the heroin somebody smuggled in to him."

David looked at his partner for a moment in disbelief. "When did this happen?" *Dammit.*

"Guard discovered him a few minutes ago. The

officers on the watch figured him dead for about
an hour before that, maybe two."

"Who visited him?"

"Nobody, that's the real pisser. He was tagged
by somebody on the inside. And it happened so
fast, whatever was in that needle was probably
laced with something. Toxicology is investigating
it now."

David stuffed the last of the files on top of his
desk inside the drawer and slammed it shut.

"What are you thinking?"

"That Jerard must have known something else
pretty good about this whole LaCrosse thing. Because sure as shit that's what got him killed."

# PART TWO

# CHAPTER EIGHT

Quade braced for the surge of water coming at him. He hurled himself to the deck, clutching frantically at the boat's wheel and controls. When the water hit, the boat surged desperately upward into the screaming wind before plunging again, nearly capsizing, almost throwing Quade into the angry swells that clawed at the hull.

No turbulent waters he'd ever sailed had been this vicious. He cursed his own arrogant underestimation of what truly was turning out to be the killer storm predicted. But he knew these waters, he tried to remind himself, had sailed them too many times to succumb to hopeless panic.

He knew that a cove offered shelter less than a quarter of a mile ahead, if only he could hang on to get there. He braced again as another angry wave of water swelled.

His luck ran out. He heard his tackle box, poles, radio, gear, all tangle along the deck in a mad jumble that crashed hard against him as the boat lurched fatally to the side. He and his possessions slammed into the churning water. Stunned, he fought the downward suction that twisted and pulled him beneath the choppy surface.

He was sinking but still had the will to thrash through his panic, to break free from the dark water. While his muscles screamed with strain and the wind above the water howled brutally, he stroked, stroked, until the black depths that clutched at him broke to reveal the hard iron-gray of the rain-soaked sky.

He would *not* die, he would not . . . and then a stunning pain streaked along his temple. A piece of hard metal debris slammed against him again before bobbing away. The wound it had inflicted burned.

His vision clouded and a strange peace beneath the water beckoned. Quade resisted . . . but everything around him started to go dark. Then darker. Everything.

"David, do you need anything before I go?"

David set aside the glass paperweight he'd been juggling. Marie leaned in the doorway of his newly finished office, waiting a bit impatiently, he thought, for an answer.

"No, take off. I was just about to go myself."

"I wouldn't, except that Jack called, frantic, about little Jack. That cold keeps hanging on."

"Then go. You put up the closed sign, right?" He put down the paperweight and made a visual check of his office to make sure that everything was straight before he followed. It had been a slow opening week and he didn't anticipate that clients were going to flock in the last business hour of the evening.

"Yeah, the sign is out, but the light is still on in front. I'll get it." She was turning to leave when the doorbell rang, surprising them both. "Well, somebody must want your help pretty urgently. Should I answer or let it go?"

"Sure, get it." David stood up. "Tell whoever it is I'll be glad to talk in the morning." Marie left and he was locking up his desk when she popped her head back inside his office, subdued.

"I think you might want to see this client," she told him.

David frowned, curious about what could have ruffled the unruffable Marie. And then the cop in him came to full alert. He touched the weapon he wore concealed beneath his lightweight summer jacket. "Is someone trying to make trouble—" He started around her.

"No, no," Marie assured him, clutching his arm. "Nothing like that. Come on out into reception. I'll lock up on my way out."

More puzzled than ever, David relaxed and switched off his desk lamp. While he followed her into the hallway, she flicked a couple of overhead lights back on as they walked. When they emerged out into reception, he saw why and forgot the lateness of the hour and his boredom.

"See you in the morning," Marie murmured, her eyes moving from him to his visitor.

David braced a shoulder against the wall, wondering what to say to the one person he had never expected to see again.

Shannon had anticipated feeling nervous, but she hadn't anticipated the other emotions that unsettled her. Seeing David again, thinking of what he had done for her, she felt grateful, beholden. And she didn't want to feel either of those emotions for anyone.

"This may be a mistake," she said, in lieu of a conventional greeting.

"It's been a long time, Shannon."

"Two months and ten days since the law let me go. See? I'm still counting."

David took his time looking her over. "Life must be agreeing with you. You look good, rested."

Shannon accepted the observation. She knew that externally, she looked whole. The body always healed.

She chose one of two visitor's chairs, sat down, looked around, and observed that David possessed something she hadn't anticipated. Very expensive taste.

The smell of fresh paint underscored the newness of his office and its decor. A pricy contemporary print here, a gleaming alabaster or brass African sculpture there—suggested a significant budget had been allotted to put his personal stamp on his space. Which made her wonder again about the change of which Marshall had informed her.

"I thought you'd committed yourself to playing the dedicated cop forever."

David shrugged. "I rarely do anything forever. How can I help you?"

"I never did thank you." She touched the strap of her purse, rearranged it in her lap.

David took the other visitor's chair, noting her unease. "I'm just glad it all worked out."

"Partly. That's why I'm here. There's more that has yet to be resolved."

Intrigued by the irony she couldn't appreciate, David urged, "I'm listening."

"Someone set me up to go to prison. I have a suspect in mind, but unfortunately, he seems to be dead."

David got up. "I know where Marie keeps the coffee. It sounds like we're both going to need some."

"Don't fetch it on my account." Shannon got up, too. "I'll help."

David changed his mind and turned back around. "Actually, I'd rather do this over food. If you don't mind," he added when she looked at him sharply. "It's been hours since lunch. How about you?"

Shannon looked at him, still wary.

"Just food," David assured her quietly, understanding. "I was thinking, a sandwich at my place, which, by the way, is conveniently the other half of this double."

"What happened to the condo?"

"I sold it." David saw how that flat statement

resurrected some unwanted and heretofore unspoken memories. For his part, he was glad one of them had brought it out in the open to at least be acknowledged if not yet dealt with.

Shannon took her time gathering her purse. "I'll just keep you company while you eat."

"Good. Let me lock up and we'll get out of here." In no time, he was ushering her outside, then back in again next door.

Modest, Shannon thought when he snapped on a light. But touched with the same smooth nouveau style that accented his office.

"Have a seat in there." He gestured to a small alcove that opened up off the narrow entryway. "I've got cold roast beef if you want to reconsider."

Shannon shook her head. "Just coffee."

David walked down the hall a bit and turned left.

Shannon discovered the alcove he had left her in was a small dining room. She sat down at a heavy, beautifully carved oak table that dominated the space. Beneath the table, she eased off one pump and then the other, and lifted a hand to her neck to knead away the stiffness.

David caught her at it but didn't comment. With their food and coffee before them, he sat down and said, "Talk." He started eating.

"I've decided someone went to a lot of work to send me to prison."

"You said you think you were framed. By whom?"

Shannon concentrated on the coffee in her mug. "I believe my husband's stepbrother, Alan Quade, set me up."

Truly surprised, David looked at her. "I've read the papers. He was killed two months ago, wasn't he, in some fishing accident?"

"Was he?"

David kept eating, but now with his eyes and attention focused fully on her. "Why do you doubt it?"

"Because Quade has never been that careless about anything, especially his own safety. And because I've learned that he was dabbling in some old business he knew I joined my husband in opposing before Peter's death."

"So?"

"So he may have had reason to think he needed me out of his way—out of Peter's life—even before Peter's death. I say this because I put together some things while I was in prison, and a few more since my release."

David noticed how her voice, her entire body, was taking on a very subtle edge. He was looking at controlled, cold fury. "Tell me more."

"Early in my marriage, Peter told me that he and Quade were approached by foreign investors representing the financial interests of high-profile clients looking to diversify their holdings to include American partners. The organization they represented is called Worldcom, Inc."

"I've heard of it."

Though the potential profit to be had from the

offer sounded good, Shannon told David, Peter's instincts had been to steer clear.

"He told me he didn't want to get involved with Worldcom because insider industry gossip claimed other American investors who came on board early during Worldcom's formation had been rumored to have racketeering links. No illegalities, however, were formally proven, or even alleged. But for Peter, the mere suggestion of illegality was enough."

"His reservations weren't shared by Quade, I take it?"

Shannon shook her head. "In fact, Quade put incredible pressure on Peter to reconsider. I, on the other hand, made it clear to Peter that I supported him in opposing Quade. Ultimately, as the controlling voice of the corporation, Peter did oppose his brother, convinced their corporate board to do the same, and that was that."

"Really?"

"Quade wasn't happy," Shannon nodded. "He was even less pleased that my opinion had impacted on Peter's decision at all."

"How did you know that?"

"Quade told me to my face." She could hear him again, telling her she'd been lucky to be the woman to actually succeed in getting Peter to walk down the aisle again. He'd accused her of using her youth and her body to get him there.

"All right. So there was no love lost between you and Quade. But aside from that, what reason do you have to believe that he might have actually set you up?"

"Motive, stemming from his resentment over a grudge he held against me for the Worldcom thing. My sister-in-law, Betty Morris, started me thinking about it when she came to visit me after I got out of prison." In fact, Shannon still felt uncomfortable with the memory of her sister-in-law's visit, the first since she'd accompanied Peter to the prison hospital.

Such an about-face from the contempt she'd spewed at the trial still made Betty an unwanted confidante in Shannon's eyes. And she wasn't at all ready to bestow on the woman the forgiveness she so desperately seemed to want. But neither was she so embittered as to not recognize that if the woman wanted to talk, she might very well be useful.

"Betty told me her brother's death precipitated the controlling interest of the company falling to her husband, Parker. Up to that point, he'd only been the LaCrosse Finance Corporation's senior legal counsel.

"But just recently, Betty confided in me that Parker has started to seriously consider an offer from European investors to bring LaCrosse Corporation's considerable interests on board with—"

"Worldcom?"

"Yes."

"Betty says two of these investors have visited their home. She even gave me their names when I asked."

"They're the ones who originally approached Peter and Quade years ago?"

"One of them is, yes."

David drank some coffee, thinking. "So your theory is, Quade had reason to want to remove you from a position of influence over Peter and their business affairs before Peter's death. And since his death, the reappearance of Worldcom suggests to you Quade's got his hands back into shaping that old merger."

Shannon leaned forward, watching him earnestly. "Well?"

"You've ruled out serendipity? I mean, Worldcom could just have been making another bid on an old prospect it still considers viable."

"Maybe," Shannon conceded. "But I find it a little convenient that a second try follows so closely on the heels of Quade's untimely death and disappearance. And then there's the other thing."

David searched her eyes, seeing that whatever this other was, was difficult.

"Peter confided something to me not long before he died." She told David about Peter's reconsideration of the foreign diversification issue, even though he hadn't elaborated on all the details. "I'd bet money that Quade started pushing him again. It makes sense. Quade wanted to invest all those years ago, and I could see then that he was never really content with the company decision not to do so."

David pushed back his chair. "You want a refill?"

Shannon held her mug and followed him into the kitchen, needing the movement.

Inside the narrow galley-style kitchen, she let him take her mug, fill it, and then top off his own. Unexpectedly, she was struck anew by what a handsome man he was. She accepted her drink and turned away from the question in his eyes when he caught her staring.

David started to follow her back to the dining room, then diverted her. "Let's go in here."

Shannon stepped aside, letting him lead the way to the living room.

From the sofa, David picked up where they had left off. "Let's talk about Quade's death." He held up a hand. "Okay, for the sake of argument, his alleged death, for now." The news reports seemed pretty indisputable."

"But if you followed closely, you know that his body still hasn't been found. He remains legally dead because his body officially remains lost at sea."

"It could have happened like that, Shannon."

"Or not."

"I presume you have some other ideas."

She shrugged. "What if Quade made a point of being seen that day, when he knew anyone's chances of surviving that predicted storm were next to impossible? What if he made a deliberate show of going fishing when he really had some other course in mind?"

"You could be reaching."

"So you thought once before, until Jerard Booley turned up."

David ignored that. "What you're saying makes an interesting argument for your *wanting* Quade to be alive, because he's got the best reason, according to your theory, to wish you out of the way."

"Are you interested in helping me prove it or disprove it? One way or the other?"

David drank some more coffee. "He's dead, Shannon."

"He is *not*." Impatient, she looked away. "Alan Quade is too mean to die," she told him. "The only way I'll accept his death is with definitive proof."

David listened to her, pondering her momentary shrillness, wondering if he really wanted to be pulled into what clearly was a precarious emotional investment for her. Testing her motivation, he murmured, "I'm not cheap, Shannon. If I accept this case, you'll pay. And you'll do as I tell you to every step of the way."

He waited for her reaction, needing to know if she would cooperate with him. But more than that, he wanted to see if the vehemence of her wants outweighed any discomfort she might have with working so closely with him.

"The money is no problem," she answered smoothly, back in control. "I can pay." So quietly that he almost missed it, she added, "I already have."

David digested that, not knowing if he was pleased or disappointed with her answer. "All right, then," he told her thoughtfully. "I accept the job. Now, this is how it'll work."

He outlined a preliminary plan. They would establish some hard facts. First, since they didn't have a body to confirm Quade's death, they had to construct an argument and evidence to support why Quade would benefit from faking his own death.

Which meant they would need to determine whether Quade truly stood to benefit from an alliance with Worldcom and, if so, how he might then theoretically influence making that happen from the "grave."

Shannon relaxed by degrees as David talked. She'd known, despite her personal misgivings about a potential alliance, that he was exactly what she needed in an ally. He was smart, aggressive, and tough. He was also more than a little skeptical, she thought, taking on the challenge of her assertions as an academic exercise. But she didn't care because deep in her heart she was convinced she could prove him wrong.

In fact, for the first time in years, she felt truly excited, energized. She was embarking on a course that would exonerate her in the public eye. She knew that social pardon, along with the legal one, would come only if Quade were alive, which seemed a ridiculous stretch.

But in her gut, the likelihood of that stretch felt

right. She said to David, "So where should we start?"

"For now, just keep your ears and eyes open. We'll refine things as we go along."

Shannon weighed what he'd just said, hearing what he'd tactfully left out. "I hope you're not suggesting that I sit back and let you take control of everything. I have a very personal stake in this and I won't sit back quietly and accept leftover crumbs from you."

"Yes, I realize how important this is to you, Shannon. That's why I'm asking you to lay low. You're running on emotion and emotion can make you sloppy."

Shannon stood up. "This is only my life we're talking about here, David. I'm searching for the justice I was robbed of two years ago—you're damned straight I'm running on emotion. All things considered, who has a better right?"

"That doesn't change the fact that everything we do has to be handled with control. Anything less could blow it all before we've even started.

"You've suggested an interesting—premise. But we can't really know what or who we're dealing with until we crawl deep inside this thing. I don't want to have to worry about you keeping your head together while that's getting done."

David's calm logic didn't dampen her determination. "I want whoever set me up, whoever was responsible for Jeff's death, brought to justice. If that person turns out to be Alan, he's going to pay."

David listened to the bitterness that had overtaken this woman whom he had once thought too fragile to bend. Maybe she was right. Maybe for that alone someone needed to pay, because prison had obviously taken from Shannon something far more lasting than her temporary loss of freedom.

"I'd better go." She got up to walk over to the hallway mirror stand where she'd set her purse.

David got up, too. Shannon stood at the door, and waited for him to unlock it, but he hesitated. He kept his hand on the knob, unable to let her go just yet.

From the moment she'd walked into his office tonight, he'd wanted to ask the question that had haunted him long after she'd married LaCrosse.

"What?" Shannon asked softly, puzzled and uneasy for reasons she couldn't pinpoint by his sudden hesitation.

David stepped closer to her, looking down into her deep, cautious eyes. "Why, Shannon? Why did you choose him?"

For a suspended moment, Shannon felt lost. Trying to regroup, she settled her purse on her shoulder and stared down at the floor. The silence stretched on between them before she answered simply, bleakly, "I needed him."

Unsettled and unsatisfied, David slowly opened the door, then closed it behind her while she walked away into the night.

# CHAPTER NINE

*Paris*

"Monsieur Arnaud, bonjour! It is a lovely day, is it not?"

The jogger didn't slow his pace, but he raised a hand to acknowledge the baker whose shop he passed each morning. The day was pristine, the air sharp and clear. "Oui, Monsieur Bette, it's glorious."

The baker wondered, not for the first time, what this man did for a living. Whatever it was obviously made the mysterious Arnaud very rich. He never went anywhere according to any apparent work schedule. And his visitors, when they weren't beautiful women, were executive types who came to him on his boat.

Ah well, it was none of his business. But still, one wondered.

Arnaud slowed as he approached his slip along the Seine. He ducked into the small yet elegant houseboat docked there and dropped onto a plush leather sofa inside his stateroom. He draped a towel he kept nearby for just this moment in the day around his neck and awaited the incoming fax he was expecting.

The machine beeped, signaling his transmission, and he tore off the single sheet with interest. He read and mused. Bad luck, the bitch being let out of prison. Worse luck, she'd evidently emerged primed for someone's blood.

Of course, that was what one had to assume, since she'd wasted no time digging the cop back up.

Arnaud contemplated the phone on the desk in front of him. She just wasn't going to let the dogs he'd worked so hard to put to sleep lie, which meant she had to be watched.

He reached for the phone, knowing who he needed to put into place to do it.

Two days later, David and Shannon were on a plane to Bangor, Maine. Their destination was the area where Quade had last been seen alive. Shannon had expected David to object to her demand to come along. She hadn't been disappointed.

She'd pushed him, arguing that it would seem perfectly plausible to the locals that the dead man's sister-in-law was fulfilling her husband's dying request to seek more substantial closure for Quade's mysterious disappearance.

David had conceded, but Shannon was reminded with every tense moment of silence that stretched between them how displeased he was that she was here.

Twenty minutes after they landed at Bangor National Airport, they were in a rental car headed for the marina from which Quade had set sail from before reportedly perishing. It was in the tiny fishing village of Millenak Harbor, forty miles southeast of the city.

As she and David cruised through the town's narrow streets, Shannon admired the brightly dressed pedestrians crowding the sidewalks. She'd missed boisterous crowds after she'd first gone to prison. Now she was vaguely aware of being glad she was safely at a distance from them, inside the car.

Shannon glanced at David a couple of times to see if he was thawing any. He still didn't say much, and so she left him to his thoughts while she wondered what their upcoming meeting would yield.

The sky was starting to cloud over by the time they pulled into the marina and David parked the car. He and Shannon got out just as a tall, thin, overall-clad man ambled out of a bait shop called Mandy's. Clearly, he was curious to investigate the newcomers and small-town enough not to care that it showed.

"How are you, folks?" He extended his hand to David, then Shannon. "Amos Mandy. How can I help you?"

Mandy was young, maybe late twenties, but Shannon still fancied he had the look of an old salt in the making.

David said, "We're here with questions about a man whose boat was lost about two months ago.

Alan Quade, from Washington, D.C. Shannon, here, is his sister-in-law."

"Oh, yes," Amos squinted, remembering. "That fellah was stubborn. Determined to have his own way, even though I warned him he was stupid—sorry ma'am, no offense—to go out fishing that day."

"But you rented him a boat anyway" Shannon said.

Amos nodded. "His money was green. Besides, he did have a small chance of not getting caught by the weather. You folks cops?"

"No," David said.

"Then why are you interested in all this now?"

"He was my husband's brother," Shannon said. "My husband recently died, but he never gave up hoping that Alan hadn't really perished. In fact, I'm here to carry out my husband's dying wish to see if there isn't something else, just one more time."

"I see," Mandy said. "Sorry for your loss."

"Yes. If only there had been a body—" Shannon looked down at the ground.

Amos pulled out a cigarette, lit it. He studied Shannon through the smoke. "Sounds like its closure you're seekin'." He turned to David. "What about you?"

David stepped closer to Shannon and draped an arm around her shoulders. "I'm a friend of the family. I don't want Shannon to do this alone."

Amos nodded again, smoked for a bit, alternately looking at Shannon and David, then out to the ocean. "Come on over here; I'll show you somethin'."

They crossed the tiny parking lot to follow Amos back to his tackle shop. Behind the shop, he led them to a dock, which sided a modest collection of motorized fishing boats. Interspersed with them were a couple of simple rowboats.

Amos pointed to a sleek little motorized beauty, moored at the end of the row. "That's twin to the one your brother-in-law took out that day. Go on over and take a look, if you want. Don't know how it'll help you, but it's about all I got that'll give you a feel for what's left over from that day."

David knelt on the dock to look inside the vessel. Standard controls for a two-seater, storage in back. "The news reports said he went out alone. Is that true?"

"Yep. That wasn't the first time he rented a boat from me, you understand. He showed up about two, three years back and kept coming regular every year."

"Alone?"

"Not always. Sometimes there was another fellah with him, about the same age. Never came into the shop, though, so I didn't get a good look at him."

"But that day, Quade wasn't with him?"

"No."

"So you couldn't possibly have mistaken him for anyone else?"

Mandy was shaking his head before David finished asking. "No, I'm sure. You two wait here a minute, I just remembered something." He left them to walk quickly back to his shop.

David looked at Shannon. She looked at the ground, clearly frustrated. The easiest explanation, a possibility of mistaken identity, was looking pretty slim. He turned to see what she was looking at when she raised her head to look over his shoulder. Mandy was coming back and he had something in his hand.

Mandy held out a Polaroid so that both David and Shannon could see. "One of the boys who lives around here asked me to take this picture of him with his big fish that morning, shortly before your friend went out. See here, this is the fisherman." He pointed to a slim, youngish-looking man posed in front of the store window.

The fisherman was holding a heavy salmon in one hand, his fishing gear in the other. Mandy's finger shifted against the photo. "Now this other guy here behind him is your fellah." Just over the fisherman's left shoulder another man had been caught in the frame.

Mandy said, "He'd just bought some additional rain gear because of the weather. See," Mandy tilted his head, drawing attention to the billed hat he wore, "he bought a hat like this. It's our own brand, only kind we sell in the store because the tourists like it. Your friend was headed outside when he walked right into the picture, here."

Shannon felt her disappointment deepen. "That's him, all right. This is Alan Quade."

David examined the unwitting subject closely. Though he was moving and slightly out of focus, his features were sharp enough, despite the red cap, to make an unmistakable identification clear.

The poles he carried, the dark rainslicker he wore, the tackle box under his arm—a typical fisherman prepared for a serious sporting day.

Shannon said, "Mr. Mandy, would you mind if I kept this snapshot? I know it probably doesn't seem like much to you, but . . ."

"To your folks back home, it's something tangible to prove Mr. Quade was here. I understand." Mandy handed over the photo.

Shannon tucked it inside her purse, then took Mandy's hand. "You don't know how helpful you've been."

"Anytime. I just wish things hadn't turned out so bad for your brother-in-law."

"Me, too. David, let's go; we're through here."

David rested his hand at the small of Shannon's back and they headed for the car.

He was pulling out of the lot when Shannon said, "I still don't believe I'm wrong. I know that seems irrational, and I don't know how Quade pulled it off. But he did not die out there in that storm."

David reached the edge of the lot and let the car idle. He assessed Shannon's stern profile. "Hitting one brick wall isn't the end. We've learned without a doubt now that it really was Quade on that boat. Now we go home and figure out what he could have gained by leaving behind his life so dramatically." He let her digest that. "I'll be in touch when I find out more."

"David—"

"Shannon, you hired me to do a job my way." He turned to her, impatient. "If you've got a problem with that, let's agree now to part ways."

Shannon sighed, trying to relax. David was right; she needed to be more patient. But understanding that and actually doing it were two different things.

Markey let the phone ring a second time, a third, and then she picked up, sounding groggy as if she'd been pulled out of bed. Markey didn't return her hello; he just let his silence and his thoughts spin out.

"Who is this?" Shannon demanded, waking up, decisive now.

Markey disconnected with a quiet click, staring past the corner pay phone where he stood. He knew what he wanted. She was there in the apartment at the end of the block, just waiting for it. She was causing trouble again, painful trouble. He thought of the emotional call he'd received just this morning. She shouldn't be allowed to live and have the chance to cause any more problems.

"Hey, Deb, how would you feel about leaving this here?" Shannon was leaning against the nearly finished playroom wall of her almost completed community center. She brushed a bead of perspiration from her temple. The air conditioning wasn't on yet and the life-sized dollhouse she'd been working on all morning, for all its dainty appearance, was heavy as lead.

Deb Molino, a petite fireball of Italian energy, tilted her head. She used the end of the paintbrush she held to scratch her arm. "What you mean is, it's staying there because it's too heavy to move."

Shannon crossed her feet as she leaned against the wall. "You got it. And, hey, it's almost noon. Isn't it time for a soda break or something?"

Deb looked approvingly at the paint job she'd just finished. "Yeah, Kit ought to be back any minute with food, including drinks. You know, this place ain't turning out half-bad, seeing as how its major construction is in the hands of a bunch of broads."

Shannon smiled, taking in the work she and her two partners had poured into the project. Peter's trust money had supplied the final capital they'd needed to purchase the acre of land the building sat on.

Was it really only two years ago that none of them had believed they'd ever see their dreams completed? And now, unpredictable fate had turned again to bring them here.

Thoughts of unpredictability roused thoughts of Quade and her trip to Maine with David. A week had passed and she hadn't yet heard a thing from him. She was finding it very hard to do as he advised: Wait and stay low.

"Shannon? Earth to Shannon?"

Shannon looked up, surprised to see Deb standing right in front of her.

"Man, wherever you disappeared to, I hope I never get there. You looked like you wanted to hit something."

"Sorry." Shannon shrugged and then she smiled, trying to throw off her dark mood for her friend.

"I guess you don't want to talk about it, right?"

"There's nothing to talk about, Deb." Shannon laid a hand on her arm. "If there were, you'd be the first to know."

"You never talk about it, Shannon. You know, prison."

Shannon dropped her hand. "There's nothing about that experience I want to resurrect or discuss."

"Oh, honey, are you sure about that? Sometimes, you look so sad."

Shannon shook her head and smiled, trying to reassure. "Then I give you permission to shake me when I do. I don't want to make you sad." She looked beyond Deb, her attention caught just then by voices in the hallway.

Deb turned to look, too. "Sounds like Kit brought somebody back."

Shannon's heart speeded up a little. She didn't need to see who was with Kit because she recognized David's voice. And then the two of them walked into the room.

"Hey, hey, where did she snag him?" Deb smiled with pure feminine appreciation. She raised an automatic hand to her hair, frowned when she remembered she'd scraped it into a ponytail for convenience, then forgot about it as Kit brought their visitor closer for introductions.

"Shannon, looks like I ran into a friend of yours. He was walking around the grounds, checking us out. So I invited him in."

"David." Shannon nodded. She introduced him to Deb and took another look at him since Deb's reaction had made it so tempting to view him through another woman's eyes.

She'd always been aware of his looks, but now for some inexplicable reason she felt as if she'd been touched by the proverbial bolt of lightning.

When they'd first met, she'd associated David with the conservative image he maintained for his job. Understated style, albeit well tailored, had defined him in her mind.

Today, as on the night she'd barged into his office, as well as their trip to the coast, he sported a very different look. She suspected it reflected the true man.

He wore a denim shirt and jeans. They hugged his long legs and were strained white in interesting places. His feet were encased not in loafers but in scuffed, expensively tooled boots. His hair was also a little longer than she'd remembered it being three years ago. In fact, there was enough of its dark waving length to fit quite attractively into the short tail he favored at his nape.

Shannon was still taking serious inventory when it occurred to her that he was taking inventory, too. Her eyes collided with his. Her breath caught when he wouldn't let her go. Only with great effort did she manage to break the contact. And she frowned.

She didn't want David Courtney to make her feel like a woman. But he did.

Kit cleared her throat. "If anyone wants lunch, I've got a bucket of chicken and potatoes, biscuits, the works." She looked at David, then back at Shannon. "You're welcome to join us, David. We're all curious to hear your opinion of what you've seen around here so far."

Shannon heard the innuendo, ignored it, and moved away from the wall to break open one of the boxes of food.

"Thanks," David murmured, following Deb and Kit over to a workbench they started clearing to use as a table. Obviously, the surprise awareness that had flared between him and Shannon had been plain to everyone. But he hadn't come here seeking it and he used the time the women took to dish up the food to surface back from his romantic haze.

As they ate, they talked about the center, the variety of kids they'd all worked with through their respective jobs, and of other inconsequential things. Halfway through the meal, Deb and Kit

were debating some point of building construction
when David leaned over to Shannon.

"Let's take a walk," he invited.

Alert to the promise in his voice, Shannon laid
down her napkin. "You guys, I'm going to give
David a private tour of the grounds."

"I'll bet," Kit murmured.

Shannon said, "We won't be long."

Deb looked over at Kit's paper plate. "You want
the rest of those fries?"

Shannon chuckled as she and David walked
out.

"They're nice girls," he commented when they
were standing on the playground.

"The best. They're the kind who don't let you
down, no matter what."

David looked her way. She was concentrating
on a row of newly planted shrubs, so he let it go.

"I think I may have made some progress," he
told her. "I've been digging around into the pedi-
gree of Worldcom, Inc. It's interesting. Thought
you might want to hear."

Shannon led the way to a swing set. She took
one of the vinyl-protected seats. David took the
one beside her.

"Go," Shannon said.

"Worldcom is an entity with many faces. Some
of them are not as amiable as others."

He explained that a friend of his from the force
had a friend working for the IRS. The IRS contact
owed David's friend a favor. David's friend had
been able to get a few records discreetly pulled.

"I've got the identities of some shield organizations whose profits seem to filter in significant quantities back to the Worldcom base."

"Where is it, Worldcom's base?"

"France. Although, a number of its newest affiliates are American."

"What about LaCrosse Corporation?"

"The name doesn't appear on its books. But that doesn't necessarily mean it's not involved somehow. There are ways other than legitimate ones to filter money into a corporate enterprise."

Shannon used a foot to gently move herself back and forth. "So what do we do next?"

"I keep digging into Worldcom. I'm going to start with a closer examination of these American corporations. If a connection with LaCrosse Corporation exists, I'll find it."

"Including the identities of the top people who are running them."

"Sure."

Shannon felt restless.

David recognized it. "I know you want to help." He started to swing a bit himself, debating. "Okay, here's what you can do. I'll give you the names of a few CEOs who I've already discovered run some of the organizations affiliated with Worldcom.

"Field them where you think they might be likely to draw a lead. Maybe your sister-in-law, Parker Morris's wife, is a good place to start, if she's still determined to be your buddy as penance.

"I wonder if I can trust her to be discreet," Shannon thought aloud.

"Probably, as long as you approach her right." David wondered if his letting her do this much was wise. And then he remembered the woman who had paced like a cat in his home, bent on making the man she believed responsible for her incarceration pay.

She'd be as careful as she needed to be.

Troubled, Shannon stared at the now-silent phone. For the second consecutive night, it had not yielded the identity of the nameless caller who had just awakened her. Instead there was only a steady anonymous dial tone. She could feel a million desperate memories rushing back and she pushed herself up against her pillows. She ruthlessly tried to quell the flashbacks and the panic.

Chances were, it had genuinely been a wrong number. After all, it was close to midnight and maybe someone had just been too embarrassed to speak up and admit a mistake.

Still, she felt a nervous moisture dampen her brow, a mental cold sweat that forced her legs over the side of the bed as she sat up. Dammit, she would *not* live her life in fear. Not when she'd just gotten her freedom back.

She needed something to drink, to soothe her. Not alcohol, she decided, padding barefoot to her kitchen, but something hot, reminiscent of her foster parents' safe home. She scanned the contents of one kitchen cabinet, then another. No coffee, no hot chocolate.

She thought for a moment, knowing the desperation she felt was irrational, but needing to soothe herself by indulging it all the same. It took her five minutes to throw on a cotton T-shirt, jeans, and loafers. Keys in hand, she let herself out of her apartment and rode the elevator down to the ground floor.

The night air was oddly clear of the humidity she knew would come seeping back with the hot summer sun of dawn. She shifted her car keys in her hand, focused on her car at the end of the walk and the five-minute drive that would get her to the twenty-four-hour grocery around the corner.

The car that came speeding out of the darkness appeared so quickly, she never had a chance to react. At first, she thought the loud noise she heard was a backfire. It wasn't until she felt a burning pain in her arm, until she registered the dark car continuing to speed away, that she looked down and saw her own blood dripping onto the walk.

A sudden wave of nausea swamped her. She'd been *shot*.

Oh, my God, she thought, dazed, managing to stumble to her car, fumble the lock, drop inside behind the wheel. The hospital, she had to get to the hospital. Somebody had wanted her to *die*.

David slammed a hand against the glass door of the emergency room entrance. He pushed it open with his full weight, almost knocking an indignant old man off balance. "Sorry," he muttered, barely breaking stride. At the registration desk, he demanded, "Shannon LaCrosse. Gunshot victim. Where is she?"

"Sir, I'll need to see some—"

David was already pulling out his investigator license and telling her that a colleague, Officer Martinez, had informed him about the shooting and was awaiting him in a treatment room. The nurse, sobered by his hard eyes and harder tone, picked up her desk phone and placed a call.

Moments later, an orderly was guiding David through white-bight corridors that smelled of disinfectant, detachment, and shadowy despair. He hated hospitals, always had. Shooting runs similar to this and more gruesome criminal follow-ups when he'd been on the job had only made his feelings worse. The orderly stopped abruptly at one of a series of open treatment room doors they passed. He gestured inside and left.

David walked in to see Jack look up from the notes he was writing. "David, man," he greeted with an almost but not quite been-there, done-that tone. He didn't need to look at David's face to know that this victim was more significant than that. "Looks like a drive-by."

David spared the briefest glance for his partner, then looked back at Shannon. She was sitting on a cot, letting a resident put the finishing touches to a bandage on her shoulder. Shannon's demeanor was calm, but her eyes still looked a little panicky. He moved close.

"Mrs. LaCrosse was lucky this was just a flesh wound," the resident said without turning or breaking the rhythm of his treatment. "Who are you," he added after a moment, "another cop?"

"A friend," David answered, deciding to ignore his irritation at the doctor's bored tone. To Shannon, he said quietly, "Are you okay?" He wanted to reach out to reassure her, to touch her in order to soothe the very faint tremors that gripped her intermittently. He knew what she was feeling. He'd experienced too many times himself those same aftershocks from sudden violence, the aftermath of fear.

But he and Shannon were years beyond the camaraderie they'd once shared so briefly, and which might have allowed her to accept his comfort.

"Somebody tried to kill me," she stated calmly. Too calmly, David thought, watching her avoid his eyes. "Is there any real chance we'll ever find out who?"

"I'll be honest, Mrs. LaCrosse," Jack answered. "Chances are slim, but a chance is always there."

"Do you have any ideas, Shannon?" David asked. "That would give us the best place to start." She looked startled and he realized belatedly that the request he thought he'd voiced so reasonably sounded more like an impatient demand. He couldn't help it. While the shooting appeared to be random, he didn't believe it for a minute.

"You mean, do I have any enemies?" Shannon smiled bitterly. "Probably hundreds, David. Surely that's not so unusual for an ex-con?"

"Now, Mrs. LaCrosse—" Jack began.

"Shannon," she interrupted calmly.

He nodded. "Shannon, don't jump to conclusions. Being defensive isn't going to let you give us the help we need to help track down your assailant. Now think carefully, honestly. Can you think of anyone who might have wanted to hurt you deliberately?"

Shannon met David's eyes, knowing her thoughts were perfectly clear to him. But his narrowed look warned her that this wasn't the time or place. "No," she answered Jack.

Jack closed his notebook. "Okay. We'll do what we can." He looked at David. "And I'll keep you posted on the progress."

The doctor stood, his treatment completed. "I'm going to prescribe some pain pills for you. They're pretty strong and may make you drowsy. I wouldn't advise driving after you take them."

"I'll have a squad car take you home," Jack told Shannon.

"No need, I'll follow her," David said before she could respond. "We'll be outside," he told Shannon, leaving her to exchange her hospital gown for her street clothes.

Outside in the corridor, he asked Jack, "What do you really think?"

Jack shrugged. "What do you? I got the distinct impression in there you two were keeping something from me."

David met his stare. "You were wrong. Do you really think this was nothing more than some punk on a random shoot?"

Jack studied his ex-partner a little bit longer, then shrugged. "Could be a gang thing, I suppose. You know what I told her in there is the truth. The chances of tracking it down with no thoughts or reasons for motive from Shannon are slim. But like I said, if something surfaces, I'll pass it on to you."

"Yeah." Just then, Shannon walked out of the room, tucking a written prescription into her hip pocket.

"Thank you, officer, for your help," she said to Jack.

"Sure, I'm just sorry this happened."

David watched both of them, worrying about Shannon. She was saying the right things but she still seemed too subdued. He took her good arm, "Come on, let's get you home."

In the parking lot, David unlocked her car for her, asked her again if she was really okay to drive, then told her to wait for him when she said yes. He jogged a few rows back to get his car.

At the curb in front of her apartment, they parked and David made it to Shannon's side of the car before she could get out alone. He shut the door behind her and told her, "I'm coming in." Shannon spared him a quick, closed look, but she didn't argue.

The ride up to her apartment was quiet. David didn't miss her decision to stay firmly on her side of the elevator compartment. Stubborn, he thought, indulging her by staying on his. When the door slid open, she preceded him out into the hallway, still without a word. Two doors down to their right, she stopped and shifted her keys, one-handed.

Taking in the lines of pain on her face, David stopped ignoring what she wanted and took the keys from her. With a look, he prompted her to quietly point out the correct key. He inserted it inside her lock then pushed open her door.

Shannon stepped inside but went no further than the foyer before she turned to him and said, without quite managing to raise her eyes above his chest, "I appreciate your coming to the hospital; you didn't have to. It's just when Officer Martinez asked about friends and relatives, for some reason yours was the first name that came to mind. A weird reflex I guess, the shock—"

"Shannon, shut up," he told her softly, and reached out to enfold her in his arms. She resisted for the briefest instant before she reluctantly relaxed. That softening was all the permission he needed to tighten his embrace, to pull her close enough so that she hesitantly curled her uninjured arm around his waist. He didn't know whether to feel bad or rewarded when this time, the words she spoke to him finally revealed her tears.

"Oh, God, I thought I had my life back, and now this. I don't believe it was an accident. It's like some nightmare that just won't end."

He laid his chin on top of her soft hair. Considering the path of vindication, maybe even retribution she had in mind, she could turn out to be more right than she knew. But that wasn't the sort of speculation she really wanted to indulge in right now.

Whether she was comfortable admitting it or not, she just wanted to be held. And so that's what he did, he held on. And experienced for maybe the first time in his life the fledgling headiness of wanting to protect somebody strictly for himself.

Shannon thought about pulling back long before she actually did. He felt so good, and he wasn't demanding anything more than this gentle trust. For so many years, it seemed she'd been looking for this kind of trust, for someone who would offer it unconditionally. No one ever had, really. Not even Peter, in the end. And so she savored the novelty of the illusion now, because that's what this was. An illusion. A chimera. How could it be anything else when she and David shared so much uneasy history between them?

At length, she pulled back and David let her go. "Are you going to be okay?" he asked, tilting up her chin so that she had to really look at him.

"Yes," she told him, feeling much more fragile than she sounded. She was turning away from him when a warm tear trickled down her cheek, surprising her. She was even more surprised when

David caught it on the tip of his finger and, with a reflective gesture she didn't think he was aware of, licked the moisture away. Then he pressed that finger softly to her lips.

It was as if, she thought, he sensed her struggling for something to say that would break the sudden tension between them. It was if he'd decided he didn't want to hear it.

And then he smiled slowly, deeply, as he backed away from her, an unreadable look in his eyes. "Lock the door behind me," he murmured.

Shannon nodded instead of speaking because the moment was too laden with things neither of them wanted to say. She pushed the door behind David's retreating back until it clicked. But it was only after she'd thrown the deadbolt above the lock that she heard his footsteps the rest of the way back to the elevators.

"Gentlemen, I believe we're done." The Iceman pushed away from the conference table. The men and women he'd addressed stood and began to mill around the elegantly appointed room. He shook hands, helping to usher them out.

He'd gotten to the last of them when his assistant walked into the room. She was clearly trying to get his attention while at the same time trying not to intrude. He unobtrusively made his way toward her.

"What is it?" He sent the last guest on his way with a pat on the back and turned to the woman.

"You have an overseas call, sir. It's the party you instructed me to put through."

"Thank you." He headed for another office. "I don't want to be disturbed."

He shut the office door behind him and settled down in his plush executive chair before he picked up his phone and transferred the call to his private line.

The voice that acknowledged him was direct, feminine, distinctly French. Her English was impeccable. "I'll put through Mr. Arnaud."

"Thank you, Melise." He waited for her to transfer the line. The routine was the same. She made the only audio contact between her party and members of his own staff.

"Hello." Arnaud's greeting was brusque. "I've received some interesting news. We've got a sudden flurry of interest in Worldcom, specifically in its holding and affiliates. Is there someone on your end who could be generating it?"

The Iceman was startled. He'd taken particular care to ensure no one would want to. "I know nothing of it. But you can be sure I'll dig into it."

"One source is already out of your way. The tax man who was free with his information for Courtney. A mugging, a robbery . . . these things happen randomly." He paused, letting the moment stretch. "You understand?"

The Iceman paused, enraged and insulted at the not-so-subtle threat. "Of course."

"Good. Report your findings to us. But don't

act on your own. Inform us first. We'll need to consider."

The Iceman chose his words. "Are you sure? Hesitating to deal with something that needs swift action could be very unwise."

"Acting hastily without proper consideration and analysis could be even more unwise. I want to know why Courtney is asking questions. If the lovely widow is in on this with him, I want to know the why behind that, too."

"All right."

The Iceman hung up after Arnaud severed the connection. An American civil servant had been killed because of Courtney. And now by association, he could be connected to another murder. Why was all of his careful layering being breached now? Surveillance had to be stepped up. He had to know what was going on.

"You what!"

Markey Shaw gripped the pencil he tapped against his kitchen table so tightly it snapped in half. He hadn't expected the rage. "You heard me. But I missed. She isn't dead."

"You idiot." Lessening anger, more concern. "Do you realize what a crazy risk you were taking? What were you thinking?"

"The same thing you obviously are or you wouldn't be jumping my shit. I think Shannon's a problem, or she's going to be. I thought you'd be glad I tried to make the problem go away."

A deep breath was taken, a bid for calm was expelled. "Are you positive she didn't see you?"

"I'm sure. I got away clean."

"Then just carry on as before. Keep her in your sights, report what seems important. I'll tell you where you go from there."

# CHAPTER TEN

One week after the shooting, David leaned unseen inside the doorway of Shannon's office. She was on the phone, her chair swiveled away from the entrance. He thought of the handful of calls he'd put in to her in lieu of personal visits. He thought of the room the distance had given them both, though he'd still called intermittently to keep tabs on her. The emotional damage from the incident seemed to be healing.

Each time he'd inquired, she'd reassured him firmly enough. But seeing her now with his own eyes gave him the relief none of her verbal responses had.

That frightened fragility that had so drawn him that night inside her apartment was submerged again beyond her habitual control. So he took advantage of the opportunity to observe her a little longer, which meant unabashedly listening to her end of her phone conversation.

"Did she say why she did it?" Shannon started to knead her brow. "How long has she been in detention?"

David's smile eased away at her seriousness.

"Yeah, I can't get away today. Tell her I'll be there tomorrow. Oh, Gloria, don't cry. You've done everything a mother could do. You're wrong. She does know. Okay." As she turned to hang up the phone, Shannon saw David. She was obviously annoyed.

"Do you get a kick out of eavesdropping on people?"

Since he couldn't deny that's what he'd been doing, he didn't try. "Is whoever you were talking to going to be all right?"

Shannon shook her head. She felt a little less irritated at his clear concern. "Probably not. Dammit. *Dammit.* Why do the worst things keep happening to the kids who really try?"

David walked inside and took the chair beside her desk. "Wanna talk?"

"There's not much really to talk about at this point. Nothing new, anyway." She sighed. "One of my old clients, a seventeen-year-old girl, who should have been preparing for her high school graduation, is being held in jail without bond on a charge of murdering her former pimp.

"She claims she asked him to let her trick for him one last time. Seems her retail job wasn't paying her well enough. So she decided she could make what she needed on her back to help fund the graduation party her mother can't afford but insists on planning anyway.

"The problem was once the trick was done and she attempted to give her pimp his cut, he decided to force a freebie from her for old times' sake. When the police took her into custody, she claimed she'd killed him in self-defense following the rape.

"The cops, given her past record, weren't really prepared to believe she'd been raped, hence the self-defense plea. Now, whichever way it turns out, the clean life she'd found is gone."

Unfortunate, David thought. But as an experienced ex-cop, he'd seen and heard of similar situations before. What was more significant to him was that despite everything that had happened to her, Shannon still wasn't quite as tough as she wanted to appear.

In fact, her agitation now just reinforced that observation, and helped him reach a decision.

She needed to know about the nasty edge this investigation into Worldcom could be taking on. He didn't for a moment believe his IRS contact was a random crime victim, just like he didn't believe Shannon had been the random victim of a drive-by. But there was no necessity to tell her just now, as long as he was on his guard. That would be enough to guarantee her immediate safety.

Additionally, the other information he'd brought for her would keep inside his pocket for a while longer. He stood up. "Take a ride with me."

"What?" Shannon had been far away in her own thoughts. Gloria wasn't the only one who concerned her. She was also worried about the other call that had preceded her friend's. A plea for help, and a surprising blast from her past.

"I said come take a ride with me. You need to get away from here for a while."

"Where?" Shannon made an effort to focus on what David was asking her.

"Does it matter? All you have to do is sit back and relax."

His invitation sounded tempting. But Shannon had lectured herself when she walked back into his life that their dealings with each other this time were going to stay strictly professional. The problem was, he still presented a very real attraction for her. Even more so since she'd experienced again the strength of his arms and their power to soothe her distress. Knowing that, she'd be foolish to go.

"What do you say, Shannon?"

"David, I just don't know if that would be wise."

"What I know," David said carefully, "is that you and I are both adults. We made our choices about each other long ago, and there are parts of the past that can't be changed. Can't we just be civil to each other? Who knows? We might even end up becoming friends."

Shannon looked away from his compelling eyes. She found his forthrightness unsettling. And challenging. If he could give their chance at friendship a second try, couldn't she do the same? She pushed away from her desk.

"All right, then. Let's go."

*     *     *

He drove past the city limits into Maryland. He didn't force conversation on her and was comfortable with her inclination to do the same. In time, the traffic thinned and dramatic rolling landscapes introduced a series of sprawling, gracious homes and mansions.

When David pulled up into the long, winding driveway of one of the latter, Shannon gave it a once-over and turned to him.

He cut the engine.

Shannon asked mildly, "You live here?"

"Not anymore. My parents spend a few weeks out of the year here."

Shannon opened her door. He'd told her long ago that his family had money. Somehow, because of who he was and what he did for a living, she'd actually forgotten. The house brought it all rushing back.

"Come on, you're allowed inside." He started walking up the drive.

Shannon had seen the smile before he'd turned around, so she didn't take offense and followed.

David used a key on his ring to let them inside.

"Won't your parents mind you waltzing some stranger into their home?"

"They're not here."

"David?" Shannon stood at the threshold.

He laughed a little and pressed his hand to her waist. "Come on, take a look around. I want you to tell me what you think."

"I can tell you that standing right here. I think it's the biggest damn house I've ever seen."

Again David chuckled and pulled her along. "How would you decorate it if you were to decide to throw a party here?"

"Are you throwing a party?"

"Uh-huh."

"What's the occasion?"

"Wedding anniversary. It'll be my parents' fortieth."

Shannon nodded. They came to what David called the solarium. Shannon had seen public greenhouses that were comparable. "Who are you inviting?" Given his parents' status, she expected the list to be impressive.

David said simply, "Lots of their friends, some of mine. My brother, his wife, their kids." He pointed out a couple of flowering hybrids and explained that his mother had cultivated them. "You could come."

Shannon stopped walking and looked at him. "Me?"

"What's the mater, haven't you ever been to a party?"

"That's not what I meant."

"Okay. Tell me what you meant."

"I thought we had an understanding before we came here, David. Socializing isn't part of it."

"Hmm, socializing. Would this—what we're doing now—fit into your definition of socializing?"

"You like being contrary, don't you?"

He smiled and urged her along. They exited into another hallway. "I'm just asking a question. I really want to know. Do you consider what we're doing right now socializing?"

With anyone else, she would have considered it hanging out. But her reaction to David, and the awareness she saw in his eyes whenever he got close to her ruled out anything that benign.

"Can't answer? Well, I call what we're doing being . . . civil. And I see no reason why we can't extend our civility to a casual setting where there'll be no pressure, no expectations."

Shannon tilted a look at him. He returned it, those dramatic eyes of his serenely bland. Shannon deliberately looked past him to a series of Japanese prints lining the corridor wall.

Was she really being overly sensitive? "If I agreed to this party of yours, when would it be?"

"This Saturday night. And in keeping with that spirit of civility, I'll even offer to pick you up."

"David," she said, not knowing what she felt compelled to warn him about.

"Yes?" He waited patiently.

Shannon lapsed into silence again.

David's mouth curved and they started walking again. He led her to the extensive grounds in the back, which were highlighted by an exquisitely sculptured garden. At its center, a lovely arc of water spouted from the tip of a stone Grecian statue.

Shannon stood on the flagstone terrace, taking it all in. As a child, she envisioned the fairy-tale palaces she'd read about in school looking much like this. It was so beautiful, and she felt acutely aware of how thoroughly David belonged to this setting and she didn't.

She'd dared to breach a monied gate before. She was still reeling from how hard she'd been smacked away.

David watched the play of emotions crossing her expressive face. He was thinking of their agreement to keep things light. He remembered how she'd loved her husband, how her apparent seclusion after his death had seemed to emphasize that.

Maybe he was being very foolish to pursue this . . . something . . . that hovered unexplored and potent between them. Maybe he was pushing something that, nevertheless, she didn't want to be there. He had an uncomfortable suspicion that he'd better determine which way he wanted to move quickly while he still had a chance to leave well enough alone.

"I'll come," Shannon said.

Too late, his inner voice told him. "Good." He squeezed her shoulder. "Cheer up, we're nice people. You'll have fun."

One of four ballplayers shooting hoops across from the community center made a shot with enough net to earn a round of congratulatory slaps on the back. He accepted the praise while he let his eyes drift over to the car pulling into the center's driveway.

The cop helped Shannon out of his car, then pulled something out of his pocket and handed it to her.

Markey touched the cellular phone inside his jacket pocket. Then again . . . He caught a pass and started maneuvering himself into position for a layup he saw opening up.

Maybe he would wait this time, see what developed.


Shannon opened her door before the doorbell's second ring. She was nervous and hoped she was appropriately dressed.

"Hi," David said, walking around her and into her apartment. She always looked good, but the chic outfit she wore took her the distance tonight. Its cinnamon hue should have clashed with her coloring. Instead, all of the rich browns and golds and reds she'd used to accessorize the short silk skirt and matching tunic made her dazzling.

"Let me get my purse, and I'll be ready," she said.

"Don't rush; we've got time." David was in no hurry to watch her long, slim, silk-encased legs leave his sight. He sighed appreciatively when she turned a corner.

Shannon leaned against the kitchen counter for a moment even after she'd retrieved her purse. With Peter, functions had usually been affairs that were formal and conservatively chaste. She'd only needed to take one look at David to know that this party wasn't going to be like any of those.

He was wearing blue, but the habitual jeans had been replaced by midnight-hued slacks, a matching unstructured jacket and vest. The silk shirt beneath was beautifully white against his brown skin. He'd broken its pristine starkness dramatically with a jewelled snap at his throat.

That adornment complemented the accessory he'd used to secure his hair, a tiny diamond that winked from a sterling silver clasp.

When Shannon rejoined him, he put down the magazine he'd been thumbing through and opened her front door. "Ready?"

Inside the car, she said, "I'm meeting Betty for lunch tomorrow to try out the names you gave me. I didn't want to go to her house, just in case Parker shows up. Not that he would during that time of day, but I—"

"Shannon, relax. It's just a friendly get-together, nothing more."

"I am relaxed," she snapped, stung at having been so obvious. She caught David's encouraging smile from the corner of her eye, but wouldn't acknowledge it. The ensuing silence lasted all the way to the Courtney estate.

The mansion was ablaze when they arrived. Shannon heard the strains of something melodic and lilting spill out into the night when the front doors opened to admit another couple who were ahead of them. The cars and limousines that lined the drive were a mixture of contemporary sports and gleaming mint classics. All in all, an impressively ostentatious display.

With Peter, Shannon had grown accustomed to the trappings of money. But even Peter had never lived or circulated in this kind of seemingly regal wealth. Why was she here? Even in her wildest dreams, this was *not* where Shannon Davis from Ernst Street belonged.

David took her hand and leaned down to whisper, "Smile, or you'll be shot at dawn."

Shannon did smile in spite of herself. It was disconcertingly easy with this David Courtney who teased her. She let him take her hand companionably in his cool firm grip, and they walked inside the house.

The senior Courtneys stood deep inside the foyer receiving their guests. Despite David's mixed heritage, Shannon could have picked out the elegant two as his parents anywhere. He shared his father's height and his lean, athletic build. Though their features were different, the handsome look of them was much the same.

David had inherited his mother's finely drawn beauty and, Shannon saw, a masculine version of her deeply lashed eyes.

"Mom, happy anniversary." David leaned down to kiss his mother's smooth, dark cheek.

"My darling." She grasped his shoulders to prolong the embrace. As David stood, his mother's eyes moved to Shannon.

"Dad." David shook his father's hand, then he turned to draw Shannon near. "This is my friend, Shannon LaCrosse."

Shannon wondered if she was the only one who

had caught the infinitesimal hesitation before David had defined her as friend.

"Shannon, my dear, it's a pleasure." Edward Courtney extended his hand and warmed the shake with a friendly smile.

She turned to David's mother. "Mrs. Courtney, congratulations." Alice Courtney offered her hand as well. Shannon took it, but thought she sensed a slight reservation in the older woman's smile.

David said, "We'll catch up with you two later. Enjoy your evening; we're going to mingle." With his hand on Shannon's waist, he led her away.

"I don't think your mother likes me." Shannon accepted a glass of wine from a waiter.

David turned to her. "Why do you say that?"

"I just get the feeling she's protective. She probably thinks you need protection from me."

"Shannon—"

"Her golden boy being seen with an ex-con and all." She shrugged, ignoring whatever he had been about to say. She took a sip from her glass and just then caught the eyes of two women across the room who suddenly broke off what they had been saying to each other as they watched her.

Busted, Shannon thought, noting their embarrassment. But even though she'd caught them obviously whispering about her, and knew that they knew it, that consolation gave her little joy.

How long would it take for everyone to start talking about her after word spread that she was here? They would all start wondering why in the hell David was escorting a convicted murderess to his parents' house.

"Shannon, look at me."

Shannon was struggling with her anxiety. The harder she fought, the harder it seemed. It took her a moment to realize David had spoken.

"What?" She turned to him then, feeling defensive, and looked past him at two well-dressed silver-haired men standing by the drawing room door. Both were looking her way. Shannon stared down at her glass.

"Not everyone knows you on sight. And in my parents' home tonight, no one is going to act like a jerk to your face."

"To my face, hmm?" She smiled sadly. "Then why are those two men over there staring me down?"

David turned to see who she was talking about. When he faced her again, he was wearing an easy smile. "Those two old rogues are diplomatic friends of my father. I've known them since I was a boy, and I'll tell you precisely why they're staring. They're envying me. They're confirmed crusty old bachelors who have come to this party together. I, on the other hand, have a very beautiful and elegant woman on my arm."

Shannon glanced back up at the two. One of them raised his glass to her. As Shannon watched his wistful expression, the cynical part of her wondered if he was curiously amused while the more rational part of her conceded that perhaps David was right.

She sighed and bit her lip. "I'm sorry. I feel foolish. I know I shouldn't be this jittery, but ever since the trial . . . and now that I'm out of prison, sometimes it just seems—" She struggled to explain.

"As if the whole world is watching you?"

Shannon nodded, unable to meet his eyes.

It was in that moment that David truly started to empathize with her hate of whoever was responsible for stealing her confidence, her pride. If by some wild stroke Alan Quade was their man, he'd see to it that Shannon had her due. And after she was finished, maybe he'd take a piece of the man, too.

"You're looking like a thundercloud, Mr. Courtney. As someone just recently told me, lighten up a little, okay?"

She was right, David thought, shaking off his dark thoughts. She needed his uncomplicated support tonight and he'd dedicated himself to giving her no less. Taking her hand again, he said, "Come on, I'll introduce you around."

The more people she met, the harder it became to reconcile the David Courtney she thought she'd known with the man so at ease with this eclectic group he called his friends. Ages, nationalities, and occupations were as widely arrayed as the clothes that sparkled and glittered on the beautiful men and women they mingled with.

Shannon met diplomats and government office workers. She met retirees and peers whose wealth cushioned them from ever having to work a day in their lives. She met as many women as she did men, and David exhibited an easy camaraderie among both.

She wondered if he suspected how many of the women gave him longing looks? She returned several of them, mentally shrugging. David Courtney was making it quite clear the he was keeping Shannon LaCrosse close to his side.

The most surprising person Shannon met, oddly enough, was David's older brother. He seemed cordial, but Shannon could tell that he was as tightly reserved as David was open. And judging from the slight tension she sensed between them, she guessed each of the brothers was fully aware of, and not entirely comfortable with, the same knowledge.

"John, turn around here for a minute." David approached behind and touched his brother's shoulders.

When John Courtney turned around, Shannon saw that he had been blocking from view a lovely dark-skinned woman David introduced as John's wife. Shannon smiled a hello at them both and they all shook hands.

Then John turned to David, giving his brother a casual once-over while he drained his glass of wine. "Good to see you again, David." He glanced over at Shannon and let the look linger a little longer than politeness dictated.

Shannon resolutely met his look and held it, head on.

John Courtney's mouth quirked before he

turned back to David. "It's been a long time since I last saw my brother the cop."

"Ex-cop," David murmured.

"Ah, yes. The latest career change. Still enamored of the footloose and fancy-free life, I see."

"Give it a rest, John. We're here to enjoy ourselves tonight."

"If memory serves, little brother, you're in the habit of enjoying yourself every night." His glance slid again, not so subtly, to Shannon.

For some inexplicable reason, Shannon found herself more intrigued than offended at this unsubtle slight. She noted with interest, however, that David seemed to be feeling more of the latter.

David said, "As usual, brother, you seem to be enjoying Dad's wine." He turned to John's wife and his tone warmed. "Emily, how're you? How are the girls?"

Emily looked worriedly from one brother to the other. "Well enough. They ask about you. You should drop by more often."

David's eyes flickered to his brother. "Maybe when I'm in the mood for a lecture. Besides, I came by to take the girls to that ball game just last week. They know where to reach me, and that I'm at their service anytime."

"I know, I just wish . . ." She met her husband's eyes. Subdued, she took his arm, letting him draw her away. "You're always welcome," she said again, then looked at Shannon. With what appeared to be an effort, she smiled. "And next time, Shannon, you come, too."

Touched and surprised by the woman's genuine warmth despite her distress, Shannon answered, "Thank you, Emily. I'll keep the invitation in mind."

"Do." Emily steered her husband away, but not before Shannon saw that the man was clearly brooding.

"So," Shannon said to David, who was guiding her out onto the terrace, "what gives with you and John?"

"It's an old story. And a boring one."

Shannon doubted if either of those assertions was the truth. For the first time during the evening, David seemed uncomfortable. She thought about letting it go, then remembered this evening was supposed to be a testing of the waters. If it was going to be possible for her and David to truly be friends, maybe it wasn't premature to start scratching a little deeper beneath David's surface.

They stopped at a stone bench in the garden. Shannon sat down. "John brought something up back there that I've been meaning to ask you about myself. We touched on it once before, but just briefly. Why *did* you choose to stop being a cop?"

David looked out at the flowers before them and shrugged. "It was time to move on."

"Funny." Shannon leaned down and plucked a blade of grass, idly scored it with her nail. "When I first met you, the strong impression I formed was that you loved being a cop. That you loved the action and the danger of the life."

"I did love the job. Well, at any rate I loved the action, as you say. But the predictability of it all finally wore thin. So I resigned and opened up my own shop."

"Is it what you expected?"

David smiled wryly. "I don't know yet, Shannon. You're my first client."

She looked up from the curling blade of grass in her hand, saw the gleam in his eye, found herself reciprocating his amusement. "Right."

David turned serious again. "What else do you want to know about me?"

Shannon considered an easy answer, then in their spirit of mutual candor told him, "I guess I'm wondering how seriously to take you." At his surprised look, she continued, "Your life, your family, all this . . . why am I really here tonight? Am I just another passing fancy?"

David was unsmiling when he answered that one. "If that were true, I would never have taken you on. You know what I'm talking about, Shannon. *That* was never a game."

# CHAPTER ELEVEN

His directness left her breathless. She'd underestimated him again. His expression was very intent. No matter how easily David Courtney laughed, he wasn't kidding now.

"What's the matter? Don't you like having the tables turned on you?"

Shannon let go of her blade of grass. "Truth time, is it?"

David cocked his head. "Your choice."

Yes, Shannon thought. It was her choice. And it was past time. She could continue to try to avoid the unresolved history between them, or she could accept the fact that she owed David.

"I know this is about Peter," she said. "And you have to understand that Peter is still very hard for me to talk about." She held up a hand, seeing his impatience. "I also know that we're long overdue for this talk."

"Okay, then. I'm listening."

"You have to know something about my life that the newspapers didn't report. I'm talking about circumstances the public wasn't able to see.

My being orphaned at ten is public record. The events leading up to that situation are not."

Shannon told David about her brother. She told him about living in a home where neither of them had known where the next meal was coming from, or even if it was coming.

She talked about Joe's allegiance to his street gang, how his loyalty led not unexpectedly to petty crime. She confessed how in her heart she still found little fault with several of the choices Joe had made.

Finally, she told David about the ugly, junkie death of her mother. "The last thing Mama said to me was the only thing that outlived her memory. She told me to watch out for myself first and foremost. For years after she and Joe died, that's exactly what I did."

He took a few minutes to digest what Shannon had told him. "But somewhere between the turbulent childhood and adulthood you must have seen the pitfalls of that insular thinking."

She ran a hand through her cropped hair. "You're right, maturity did much to open my mind. When I got into social work, I told myself I was going to do whatever it took to save one or a handful or a dozen kids who had been as lost as I was. The toll that commitment takes hasn't turned out like I expected."

David remembered her asking him about his own professional choices. *"Is it what you thought it would be?"* He hadn't really understood what she was saying. He'd tossed off a frivolous answer instead of the more serious one she might have deserved.

Shannon was saying, "I just started feeling like too many of my cases were just delays to failure. So many of those kids who didn't make it weren't the bad ones, David.

"It just started to seem like the more I got involved, the more I saw that some people seemed doomed to never get a break, no matter how hard they tried. For every kid I helped, I lost two others." She took a deep breath and added softly, "It got me to wondering when Shannon Davis's street destiny was going to catch up with Shannon Crosby, the foster kid who'd made good."

"But Shannon, you did get out. You achieved for yourself what dozens of those kids you grew up with and counseled didn't dig deep enough to find the strength to do. You got an education and fought to leave the drugs and poverty and anger from your inner-city childhood behind. You forged your own destiny."

"I tried. But maybe ending up in prison just confirmed what I feared all along, that everything good that happened to me wasn't really meant to be."

David guessed where this insecurity was going. He looked out over the lawn. "And so you met Peter LaCrosse."

"Through his son. I'd known Jeff long before he introduced me to Peter. Jeff and I had become good friends way before I even started conceptualizing my community center. But that's what motivated his offer to put me in line for his father's financial backing.

"I was reluctant, but there was Mama's voice in the back of my head. And Peter was so sweet about it, so sincere . . ."

David heard her husky emotionalism and tried not to feel jealous of an honorable man who had died.

Shannon cleared her throat. "The kicker to the whole situation was that Peter and I honestly were attracted to one another. We married, and for the first year it was really, really good." She trailed off. "You know the rest."

"Not quite, Shannon. Somewhere in there you met me."

Shannon took her time answering. "I can't justify almost sleeping with you that night. I was confused about it afterward, sorry for how I'd misled you to that point. In a way, an important way, a part of me always felt that I had been unfaithful to Peter, even though you and I never did anything wrong."

And why was that, David thought, frustrated?

As if she found it hard to say, Shannon continued, "I did marry him, in part, for the security he offered. And yes, his money by definition was part of that. But I never married him only because I wanted the material advantages LaCrosse money could buy. I just needed somebody older, solid, like Peter LaCrosse, at that point in my life."

David looked closely at her in the fading afternoon light. "So how do you explain you and me?"

Shannon shook her head. "You scare me, David Courtney. With you, I feel as if I'm never really fully in control."

Yes, he knew that, understood it, because with her he felt the same.

He rested his elbows on his knees and studied his clasped hands. "So where do we go from here?"

"I don't know. My life is still unsettled. This . . . thing," she said, "with Quade is something I have to see through first."

David nodded; he had realized that. And for his part, he had to decide just how deeply he really wanted to get involved with Shannon in spite of that, or maybe because of it.

She had been running on full throttle for so much of her life, maybe she didn't know how to slow down. Maybe she was a bad risk. Could he honestly fit into her life when she was so consumed by this whole prison experience? "Come on," he said, getting up. "I'll take you home."

Shannon joined him and neither said a word all the way back to the house.

That night in bed, David thought long and hard about what he and Shannon had said to each other. He'd uncovered a troubled depth in her that he hadn't expected. But what she thought were her weaknesses he viewed as strengths. If she'd really been ruled by the fear she'd talked about, she never would have made it past the huge disadvantages she was born into.

She never would have succeeded in lifting herself out of poverty through the power of her intellect and her sensitivity. She wouldn't ever have cared too much, as she still did, for the bad clients as well as the good whom she chose to devote her energies to.

And most of all, she would not have been as hell-bent to find restitution not only for herself, but also for the memory of a good friend and his father, her dead husband.

David clasped his hands between his pillow and his head. So what did he want from Shannon La-Crosse that she was realistically capable of, if not yet willing to give? A relationship? Yes, he thought he might.

But after tonight he knew Shannon wasn't a woman who would accept a nonplatonic relationship lightly. She'd loved and been loved once. She wouldn't settle for anything less than the emotional security that relationship had given her.

And honestly, he thought, the truth was she didn't deserve to. Feeling as if something had been settled in his own mind, David turned over and went to sleep.

The next afternoon, Shannon met Betty Morris at a trendy little seafood restaurant at Washington Harbor. Shannon arrived early and signaled the older woman across the room when she arrived.

"Thanks for coming, Betty. I realize you didn't have to."

Betty seated herself and fastidiously spread her

napkin in her lap before she picked up her menu. "It wasn't any trouble, Shannon. Not when you sounded so urgent."

Shannon digested that. "Let's order now and have our discussion later," she suggested.

Betty agreed. Over their meals, they talked about inconsequentials. Shannon would have found Betty's chatter hard going had it not become clear to her how lonely the woman was. In spite of herself, she felt sympathy for the woman. Parker, apparently, was not as attentive a husband as he could be. And the only other outlet for her affection, her nephew Jeff, was gone.

When their dishes had been cleared away and they sipped iced tea, Shannon attempted to elicit the information for which she had come.

"I've been wanting to know, Betty, how is Parker getting along with the business?" At Betty's surprised look, Shannon added, "You're the only one I feel I can ask about that. Parker and I were hardly on good terms the last time we spoke."

"Why do you want to know?" Clearly, Betty wasn't completely comfortable talking about her husband's job.

"For Peter's sake." That wasn't untrue. "The company meant so much to him, and he meant so much to me. I can't help but to be concerned about it." And she was for Peter's sake—despite the fact that he'd left her nothing of it as an inheritance. His ambivalence about her had endured to the end, clearly judging her trust fund enough.

Betty seemed to relax again. "In fact, Parker seems to be doing wonderfully well at the helm." She smiled. "For a man who always considered himself a lawyer first and a corporate dynamo last, that is."

Uh-hm, Shannon thought, smiling with her. "Yes, I know Peter valued him highly. Tell me, whatever happened to that big international deal you mentioned a while back, the one that involved the European investors?"

"What about it?" Betty was cautious now.

"Did it happen? Did Parker end up doing business with—what was it?—Worldcom?"

"I don't really know much more than I've already told you about it, Shannon."

"Really? It was potentially a pretty big deal, wasn't it? Doesn't Parker confide in you?"

"Of course he confides."

Shannon backed off. She sipped her tea. In the ensuing quiet between them, Betty seemed to deflate a little. "The truth is, he doesn't confide everything in me, but then what wife really expects her husband to? He's asked me to host some investors at dinner once or twice, and I have."

"So in all likelihood, things are proceeding."

"Probably, yes. But I honestly don't know the details of the venture."

"Okay. There was something else I wanted to ask you. Going through some of Peter's things—letters, journals, other personal items—I ran across the names of a handful of old friends of his. I believe he met them through a young business associate, but I can remember him occasionally mentioning them to me now by name. I wonder if you'd recognize any of them, or know how I can get in touch."

"Why?"

"Because I'd like to reminisce with them about Peter, I guess."

Betty shrugged. "I'm not sure that I'd know anybody like you mean. Parker pretty much only handled the legal business for the company while Peter was alive. I was just his wife."

"I understand. Nevertheless, I've written some names down. Would you look at them, see if any are familiar to you?"

"I guess, okay."

Shannon reached inside her purse and withdrew David's typewritten list. She pushed it across the table to Betty.

Betty scanned the names and Shannon's hopes waned as Betty made her way down the list, clearly recognizing none of them. But then she started tracking some names that appeared at the bottom with her finger.

Shannon leaned forward. "What?"

"Well, these two here, Martin Hanna and Tom Pierce. I do know them from somewhere. I've heard their names before."

"Yes?"

Betty scratched her ear and peered off into the distance, trying to recall. "Now and then at dinner with Peter." A thought struck her. "They were young businessmen, all of them. Things for Peter and Alan took off first, though—that's why Hanna and Pierce often consulted them for start-up advice."

"So, all of you were close back then?"

"Oh, I don't know if close is the right word. But we were all . . . very well acquainted."

"What happened to Hanna and Pierce?"

"After a while, the dinners ceased. Hanna and Pierce just sort of faded out of the picture as far as I could tell. I never really had reason afterward to ask about them, and Peter and Alan stopped mentioning anything about them." She shrugged. "I just assumed they must have gone into some other business venture and done all right."

Shannon accepted the list Betty slid back to her. She folded it and tucked it inside her purse. "Well, maybe I'll try to look them up someday. It would be good to hear whatever memories they can share about that early part of Peter's past."

Betty looked concerned. "How are you doing, Shannon, really? I've wanted to know, but considering . . . I didn't think you'd welcome my asking."

Yes, considering, Betty was actually right. But Betty had also just demonstrated that she could be useful. "I remember the good times, Betty. That helps me make it through."

"Good, I'm glad." She offered a smile that seemed relieved. "By the way, I've been reading about your community center. Is that what you're going to do full-time now?"

They chatted a bit longer about Shannon's plans for the facility. But Shannon was responding only halfheartedly. She was eager to tell David about the connection between Peter, Alan, Parker, and two of the Worldcom-affiliated names.

When a natural break in the conversation arose, Shannon gathered her purse, signaling to Betty that she was ready to go.

"There is one thing, Betty, a favor I'd like to ask of you," she told the older woman on their way out.

"If I can. What is it?"

"I'd appreciate your not letting Parker in on my questions about the business. He wouldn't appreciate my asking and I'd just as soon avoid causing that sort of unpleasantness between us."

"Yes, you're probably right. I won't say anything."

Shannon smiled more easily, trusting the earnestness in Betty's eyes. "Thanks. And that goes for the company, too."

At the restaurant entrance, Betty laid a hand on her arm. "If there's anything else I can do to help you, even if it's only to provide company, you'll let me know, won't you?"

Shannon looked into the woman's pleading eyes, wanting to respond to her loneliness. But it was still too soon and maybe always would be. She tucked her hands inside her coat pockets. "Bye, Betty." She turned from the woman's uncertain smile and walked away.

*    *    *

Markey pulled away from the curb fronting the riverside plaza. He debated internally while Betty Morris walked past, oblivious to him. So she was getting chummy with Shannon. Why now? What was she up to?

Damn. Should he say anything about it? *Damn.* Then he remembered his new resolve.

On her drive back home, Shannon considered her relationship with Betty. There probably wasn't much more her sister-in-law could do to add to the information Shannon sought. But she herself was privy to other sources of information for which she didn't need Betty's involvement. Old neighborhood ties, neighborhood blood. If she tapped into them now, if she extended her inquiries about Hanna and Pierce, she could reclaim some control of this investigation.

And if her own efforts yielded results, well, she'd inform David about whatever was necessary for him to know.

As she pulled up to the center, she impulsively decided to call it a day. The meeting with Betty, the effort at ingenuous cordiality had taken something out of her she didn't have the energy to try to reclaim. Taking some necessary paperwork home sounded infinitely appealing.

She was preoccupied with figuring out what she needed when she stepped inside her office doorway and saw the rose on her desk blotter. Her heart gave a funny little jolt as she reached over the flower to pick up and read the attached note:

I want to have lunch with you tomorrow.
Noon. Be ready.

David

Shannon smiled a little, remembering the cautious comfort they'd found with each other the last time they'd been together. She smelled the lush, red petals of David's rose, then carefully tucked his note inside her briefcase along with the files she collected.

# CHAPTER TWELVE

"Okay, that's good." David looked at the two names he'd just taken from Shannon to copy down inside a small notebook he tucked back in his hip pocket. "Was that all she could tell you about Hanna and Pierce?" He stretched back on the grass, enjoying the green little oasis he'd staked out along the Mall for their picnic.

"Yeah. This is good, isn't it? Now we have a connection between this cartel, Peter and Alan, and maybe LaCrosse Corporation."

"Yeah, this would appear to be a link. But don't get excited yet. I'll need to check some things out."

Shannon made a sound of agreement, but her attention had turned to a volleyball game being played with much laughter and great ferocity by some teenaged boys who'd erected a net a little further down the grassy concourse.

From their picnic spot, they had a direct view of the Smithsonian and the hundreds of school-children, and tourists pouring in and out of it. Juice, ice cream, and hot dog vendors made change and dabbed sweat with equal dexterity. All in all, it was a picture-perfect summer afternoon.

David had hoped his rose would preface a getaway during which neither of them would think about Quade, Worldcom, or conspiracies. Maybe they could take another look at the trust that had begun to spring up between them at his parents' party. But judging from Shannon's seriousness, he'd been wrong.

She looked so pensive, maybe even a little lost.

He'd gotten a buzz from the street he suspected could shed some insight into the shooting. It seemed although Markey Shaw had pretty much been invisible after Booley had given his name up in connection to Shannon, he had now resurfaced.

David had considered sharing that news with Shannon. But he'd learned she'd grown up with Markey, and he knew she trusted her memory of their friendship over anything he could tell her about Jerard, and how he'd implicated Shaw in her frame-up. At least not without proof.

Given that, he couldn't share his suspicions about Shaw until he followed up a related lead he was working on.

But the shooting was only one part of what he was sure weighed heavy on her. Prison was the other.

He could only guess at what had gone on, beyond the details he knew, inside prison walls. But his imagination, stoked by his law-enforcement insight, easily heightened his sense of outrage every time he thought of her experience.

The Shannon he had first met all those years ago, first known . . . first felt stirrings of affection for . . . was not the creature of unrest who sat so beautiful and still before him.

Just then, she turned her head against her knee and looked his way.

"Why are you brooding?" she asked.

David shrugged a little. "Why are you?"

"I'm sorry if I don't look like I'm having a good time. I am." She leaned back until her weight was supported by her outstretched arms. "Getting away, mingling, it's exactly what I needed. You were sweet to suggest it."

"Then come over here and tell me that."

Shannon was slow to swing her gaze around to his, and when she did it held definite reservation.

"Shannon, I think you know by now I won't bite. I just want you to come closer."

After a moment, Shannon shifted a little and scooted along the blanket until she was within his reach.

David looked deeply into her eyes while he reached out to caress her hand. "I want to ask you a simple question."

"Okay." Almost shyly, she tucked a windblown strand of hair behind her ear.

David followed the gesture, remembered how soft that hair had felt against his lips. "How would you like to go have some fun with me tonight? A little music, maybe some dancing."

"Well." She stared down at their blanket.

David pushed the picnic basket aside. "What is there to consider, Shannon? Just do it. It's time you started giving yourself permission to have fun again."

Her eyes lifted to his, a little startled.

He was pleased with her reaction. "My treat."

"Does this invitation fall under the category of civil behavior?" she asked after a moment.

Though he was delighted with her teasing, he didn't answer right away. They both knew the fragility of what they were feeling was still too fraught with possibilities for mistakes.

He wanted that discomfort gone; he wanted to reestablish the level playing ground their relationship had begun on so long ago. "Characterize my invitation however you will, Shannon. I just want to take you out."

Shannon nodded. "If I agree, what then?"

"Then we take things one step at time. The important thing is, I think we both really want to do this. Am I wrong?"

"No, you're not. But slowly; we take this slowly."

David relaxed, feeling relieved. "So, I'll pick you up at eight tonight. Oh, and Shannon?"

"Yeah?"

"Dress comfortably, and I won't mind if you wear something kind of hot."

Shannon was still smiling as they got up to gather their dishes to leave.

\*    \*    \*

He took her to a little jazz club that was a favorite of his. She didn't disappoint him with her response to his request, either. Her soft silver jersey tank coordinated with lovely ease over a matching thigh-high skirt.

As they walked into the dim interior of the establishment, he had the satisfaction of watching other guys' eyes follow what he knew only he was going to get to touch.

The band was between sets and David and Shannon stood at the door until they were greeted by an attractive waitress. Shannon was amused when the girl put on an extra bright smile for David.

She could sympathize. He was wearing the habitual jeans. But tonight they were black, slim, and stylishly molded to his powerful legs. The shirt he'd paired them with was pewter silk, a dramatic foil against his dark skin and the silver clasp at his nape.

They were shown to a table just off the center of the stage, toward the back. When Shannon had agreed to come out with David, she somehow hadn't expected to end up anywhere where they'd be sharing their intimate space with other couples. But the closeness of the room necessitated just that.

She loved it, Shannon thought, taking a seat and nodding at an inaudible round of hellos. While she felt exclusively connected to David, she liked being able to share that good feeling with a relaxed young group, obviously set on having fun.

She turned to David at the end of a particularly impressive instrumental solo. His intimate wink told her he was enjoying himself with her. The last of her predate nerves faded away. David signaled for another round of beers, then draped an arm across her shoulder. Shannon settled back against him, enjoying the way he took charge.

The band started up again and Shannon tapped her foot with the beat. It had been so long since she'd done something so simple as this with friends her age. And she used to do it quite a bit before she met and married Peter.

In fact, Peter hadn't really enjoyed the crowds or noise of these sorts of places. More formality, preferably the supper club milieu, had been his style.

Shannon realized only now how much she'd missed acting like the young woman she was.

Though the band and crowd were really good tonight, David felt like breaking out three sets into the evening. He leaned forward to suggest moving on to Shannon.

"Where?" she mouthed over her shoulder, right against his ear in deference to the volume of the music. He shivered a little at the feel of her warm breath against his skin. "To another little place I know."

Shannon picked up her purse and let David lead the way.

As they pulled up to a riverside dock she realized she had expected a different venue, again with more people. Clearly, that wasn't going to be the case. David helped her out of the car and across the parking lot that bordered the pier.

The yacht moored there was their destination, it seemed, and somehow, Shannon wasn't surprised. But the sudden intimacy that suggested put her a little on edge again.

"Yours?" She held his hand as he ushered her aboard.

"Yep. I get away from work now and then. When I do, this is one of the toys I like to play with." He asked softly, "Is it all right?"

"It's different," she prevaricated. "I've never been on one before."

David nodded, noticing how deftly she had sidestepped his question. On board, he watched her walk to the railing while he excused himself to confer with Ned, the chef he'd shanghaied from his parents for the evening.

He was content to let her set the pace they'd follow because he didn't want to lose the ground he'd already won tonight.

Shannon folded her arms along the railing. She closed her eyes, thinking, and let the warm night air flirt against her face.

Two years ago, David had been relegated, by circumstance and misunderstanding, to the position of Shannon's adversary. An evening like this hadn't been even within the realm of imagination for either of them.

And now, here they were together again under the guise of budding friends, maybe even something more. Destiny was a strange thing. She leaned a little further into the breeze and started when his hand touched her shoulder.

"Can I share?" He moved around her to fold his arms and lean along the rail beside her.

"What do you want to share?" She smiled easily before she knew it. He really was a very beautiful man.

"Those deep thoughts that are keeping you over there, far away from me."

Her smile broadened before fading. "I was just thinking how odd fate is."

David turned so that the warm metal supporting his arms was behind his back. By decklight, he studied her pensive face. "Tell me about it, Shannon. Tell me about prison." He really hadn't intended to ask, but he sensed it was part of what she was talking about. It certainly was a part of her experience he was hoping more and more she would open up to him.

In her mind's eye, Shannon absorbed his question and saw again the confining walls, the neutral colors, the wire fences. She smelled the sterile air, felt the isolation of her mind as well as her soul. She thought of Rose and her overture of friendship that had really been a prelude to betrayal.

"It's not something I talk about, David. I just want it behind me. Over."

Well, it's hardly that, David thought, watching the quiet emotion sadden her face. Despite what she said, she couldn't let go. But, he reluctantly agreed, that wasn't something they had to deal with tonight.

After all, he hadn't brought her here to make her sad. Quite the contrary. He took her hand. "Come on, I'm sure dinner is served."

Shannon permitted their uniformed—her eyebrow rose—server to seat her while David took the chair opposite her.

Crystal and silver adorned the snowy linen-covered table. Shannon arranged her napkin in her lap, admiring her beautifully presented dinner. A golden braised chicken breast was the centerpiece of a palette complemented by an abundance of fluffy wild rice. She selected a warm roll from the basket between them.

"This is all very elegant. You lead quite the double life, Mr. Courtney."

David shrugged and winked good-naturedly. "Why, whatever do you mean, Ms. LaCrosse?"

She smiled back. "Grit and denim by day. Silk and elegance by night. Will the real David Courtney please stand up?" She bit into her roll, watching him.

"Why does one have to negate the other? Maybe I'm really what I seem. Both." He pulled a bottle of wine from an ice bucket at his elbow and poured them each a glass.

"You're very different from your family, aren't you?"

"So they delight in telling me."

Shannon detected some wickedness. "And you enjoy supplying the ammunition that allows them to keep doing it."

"Yeah, you're probably right."

"Just a rebel at heart?"

"Just someone determined at all costs to be his own man."

"That's been a problem?" Shannon pressed the opportunity she sensed.

"Not when they've got John to fill in the gap."

"Be serious."

"I am."

Shannon looked away from him and quietly ate.

David glanced up at her now and then, knew she was waiting him out. The longer the silence stretched between them, the more it occurred to him that despite his knee-jerk reticence, maybe he did want to talk. Still reluctant but compelled to speak, he said slowly, "Dad and Mom wanted me to go into law."

"You did," Shannon said after a moment of silence.

"No. They wanted something more white collar for their son than crime fighting."

"So they pressured you."

"Maybe. All I knew was that even then I didn't like being pushed. I fell in, as they say, with a questionable crowd."

"We're close to the same age and the city isn't that big," Shannon commented. "I never heard of you before we met as adults."

David understood perfectly what Shannon was saying. The tourist guides liked to tell Washington's visitors that D.C. was a "city of trees." David's experience was that while that pretty claim was true, it was equally true that inner-city D.C. was a city of streets.

Where you grew up, who you grew up with marked you, gave you recognition, shaped the person you'd probably turn out to be. Some of those ways could be indelible. "My gang ran around opposite your end of town," he told Shannon. "We were probably into a lot of the same drugs, alcohol, stuff you encountered growing up. We just had the means to do it a bit more genteelly."

No doubt, Shannon thought. "So what put you onto the straight and narrow?"

"My respect for my parents. The self-respect they instilled in me. It all won out over a montage of friends and experimentation that showed me how completely hell-raising led to nowhere. There was no future in where I was headed."

"But you were still looking for direction. How did you find it?"

He laughed. "There was this cop I had a—let's say an *intimate*—acquaintance with. Actually, he knew my dad before he got to know me. They were friends, which probably had much to do with his intervening in my life.

"He basically pulled me aside and laid down the law one day. Literally. What he said stuck. I started seriously looking into the other side of law enforcement, liked what I saw, and didn't turn back."

"But still, now you've given it up."

David swirled the wine in his glass as he considered his answer. "I gave up the routine of it, the regimentation. I didn't throw away the essence of what I did. It's what I still do."

"Try to catch the bad guys?"

David let his eyes settle on hers. "Try to impose some justice, maybe closure for people who can't do it so easily on their own."

Shannon thought about that. "Is that philosophy behind what inspired you to get involved again with my problems? With me?"

"You're not a cause, Shannon," David said carefully but firmly. "I got involved because I felt that becoming a part of what you symbolized for me now is—right. I wanted to be with you tonight, here like this, because I'm hoping you're feeling the same way."

She was, and it scared her. Over the years she'd put so must trust in people who, in the end, hadn't deserved it. "I'm just starting to feel as if I'm getting my feet back under me, David."

He drained his glass. "We've both made some mistakes with each other. But maybe we're both ready to close that chapter of the past, to start healing the destruction."

"Maybe."

"All right." He pushed back his chair and walked around the table to take her hand.

Shannon let him guide her over to a couple of loungers. Before she could choose one and recline, he held her in front of him. "I know whatever road we take together probably won't be easy. But I'm ready to try."

Shannon rested her hands on his shoulders and let herself be pulled gently into his arms. She ducked her head and nervously studied the top button of his collar. "I think . . . so am I."

David tipped her chin up and kissed her. The contact was patient, soft, and when he let her go he smiled encouragingly into her eyes. "Well, we're a damn sight further along than we ever were in the past, aren't we? We can't do any better than to try."

# CHAPTER THIRTEEN

"Deb, your family has been around here a pretty long time, haven't they?" Shannon leaned on the broom she'd been using to sweep the rec room floor.

"All my life." Deb shook out a dust rag. "Why?"

"I'm curious about a couple of guys who may have lived around here when we were kids. They're older than us. In fact, they're probably closer to our parents' ages. Guys named Martin Hanna and Tom Pierce."

Deb thought about it. "Neither of them sound familiar. Why do you want to know?"

Shannon had no intentions of telling her the real truth. "They used to know Peter. I've had the urge, lately, to connect with some of his friends I never really got the chance to know."

Deb nodded, looking concerned. "It brings you closer to him, doesn't it? Honey, I wish I could help you. Listen, why don't I ask my parents? If either of those guys lived around here, they'd know something."

"Know what?"

Both Shannon and Deb turned to their new handyman, lounging in the playroom doorway. Who would have thought Markey Shaw would turn up after all these years? And on her doorstep, no less, asking for a job he looked like he needed badly.

Besides having done a good deed in hiring him, Shannon liked the happy memories from her childhood that he brought with him. She remembered that even as kids, Markey had been drawn to her because she didn't swat him away like many of the other kids.

He'd seemed kind of pathetic to her, and his loneliness had made a bond to the inner neglect she'd suffered at the time. Which was why impulse—and the ear he still had to the streets—urged her to reach out to him now.

She explained about Hanna and Pierce. "Of course, they would have been way before our time, Markey."

Markey shrugged, looking thoughtful. "I'll have to think about it, but I stopped by to show you something. There's some loose concrete on those new steps off the back door. I need to make some repairs, I'd like your advice on the positioning. Can you spare a minute?"

"Well, sure," Shannon answered, disconcerted by his abrupt dismissal of her question. She wiped her dusty hands on her jeans. "Deb, I'll be right back."

Deb went back to dusting.

At the building's rear entrance, Markey held the door open for Shannon. Outside, he hopped down a couple of steps and sat. At the silent invitation, Shannon joined him, puzzled.

"Shannon, I didn't want Deb to overhear us."

Intrigued by his seriousness when he was normally so low key, she commented, "That sounds ominous."

"So did your question back there. What are you into?"

Now Shannon turned wary at the way he looked her in the eye. "Why do you want to know?"

Markey watched a few cars at the bottom of the lot drive past. "I've been hearing some things on the street about you. Things that other people are going to a lot of trouble to make sure you don't find out about."

"What's this about, Markey?"

He looked at her again, thinking about his change of heart, knowing he could be making a deadly mistake. "I just said. It's about you. And Jeff LaCrosse, and that whole bad rap you fell into. I can't explain, but I can tell you you're being watched."

Shannon was startled. Involuntarily, she swept her gaze over the yard. There was nothing but the crisp green landscaping she'd paid a small fortune to have installed.

"You won't see nothing out there, Shannon. I know."

She turned back to him. "I'm afraid to ask how, Markey."

He folded his arms across his knees. "Then don't. If I was your enemy, would we be sitting here?"

Unsettled, Shannon didn't know what to think. She stood up. "Have you been asked to spy on me, Markey?"

Markey still hadn't figured out everything, and for that reason chose to withhold some information for the time being. "That doesn't matter. I just wanted to tell you this. You've got enemies, Shannon. But ain't a lot of them in this neighborhood.

"Folks around here know what you've done for them and what you're still trying to do. I know, I've seen. And we know how to look out for our own. So I think I might be able to get you some information about those two dudes you was askin' Deb about. Give me some time on it, okay?"

"Markey—"

"And in the meantime, just hang loose. I'm looking out for you, and I think that cop of yours is, too."

"What do you know abut David?"

"He's the man, but he's a good dude." Markey stood up.

Shannon watched him go back inside, and as the door closed behind him wondered what she should do. She hadn't wanted to involve David in her own street inquiries unless and until they yielded something productive. But based on what

Markey had just told her, maybe keeping what she'd just found out to herself was unwise.

Maybe she should confide in him for the sake of his safety as well as for her own. She stood inside the doorway hesitating.

On the other hand, why would Markey have told her what he had if he wasn't being sincere about having her best interests at heart?

She walked back inside. She'd give it a little while longer, see what Markey turned up. She was on her guard now, and being aware would keep her as alert as she needed to be to accumulate something useful to bring to David other than premature fear.

Shannon, in fact, was very much on David's mind as he pulled his car into the center's parking lot. Their date and the time he'd spent with her had him feeling very good, optimistic. He scooped the bouquet of roses off his passenger seat and got out of the car.

"Wow, are those for me, good-looking?" Deb stood in the entrance from where she'd noticed David's arrival.

David smiled, recognizing a kindred flirt. "Next time, doll. Where's Shannon?"

"Out back looking at steps."

"No she's not, she's right here." Shannon stepped around Deb and smiled at David. Then she saw the flowers. "What have you done?"

"Followed an impulse, continued where we left

off." Despite Deb's avid attention, David leaned forward to give Shannon a kiss.

The moment his lips touched hers, Shannon forgot Deb, too. She walked outside, instead, to join him on the porch. "We'll be back," she murmured, then she accepted her flowers in one hand and took David's hand with her other.

They meandered to the swing set on the playground out back. Taking her roses from her, David set them carefully on the ground, then settled her into one of the swings. Gently, he started to push. Shannon closed her eyes.

She concentrated on the warm sun against her eyelids, the slight moisture in the breeze she knew would later turn uncomfortably damp. At this moment, everything seemed just right.

She loved the physical rush of being pushed higher and higher in the swing, and then the sensation of coming to rest over and over, safely in David's arms.

Then gradually, the motion slowed. By the time it stopped, David was standing in front of her, waiting for her to open her eyes.

She watched his large hands engulf hers on either side of the chain linked ropes that supported her weight. She sighed as he leaned toward her, on the brink of a kiss. "I'm sorry, Shannon," he whispered, "for everything. For not believing in you, for prison, for everything you lost to that place."

Startled, then unbearably touched, Shannon closed her eyes, overwhelmed.

"Don't cry." He used his hands to cup her head, to hold her still while he dropped a kiss to her forehead. "I'll make it up to you . . . let me make it up . . ."

Shannon emitted a soft sound as David's lips drifted down to settle on hers. Her hands tightened around the metal ropes of the swing when the tentative touch of his tongue asked her for permission to take more. Something cold that had been lodged inside her for so long began to shift.

David trailed his hands from her temples to the soft skin of her throat, then down further to the cool, smooth skin of her bare shoulders. With the lightest of tugs, he pulled her up from the swing to enfold her more completely in his arms.

Shannon looped her hands around his waist, letting her body press flush against his. Somewhere on the edge of her consciousness, she knew that to onlookers what they were sharing probably appeared tame.

What she was feeling in her heart wasn't. David was aroused, there was no mistaking it from the tension in his hands to the very male part of him he gently rubbed against her.

There was no mistaking her own excitement from the short little breaths that were all she could catch when his mouth detoured to taste her throat. She may have whispered his name. She knew he whispered hers when she felt the expulsion of his warm breath against her jaw just before his mouth took hers again.

Had she ever felt this immersed in a kiss? Had

she ever felt this restlessness for the total pleasure of which David was only giving her a hint?

A crow cried mournfully somewhere above them. The distraction gave Shannon strength to pull back even as everything in her body clamored for his.

She felt David tremble a little, a touching vulnerability that coaxed her back into a hug that was as close as what they'd just shared. "May I see you tonight?" he asked her.

Shannon closed her eyes. They'd already made so many mistakes with each other. She wanted desperately to do what would be right for them now. "Oh, David, I don't know."

He probably had his answer in her inability to tell him no, he thought. The question was, did he have the courage to take what they both wanted? She was leaving the decision to him. He very much wanted to rise above his own needs this time to attempt to do what was best for them both.

He needed to think but he couldn't as long as he held her. And so he let her go and knelt to retrieve her flowers.

Shannon watched his bent head, serious, respecting his silence. Softly she stated, "I think we've played this particular scene before, although my flowers aren't nearly so wilted this time."

David straightened to his full height, looming over her. "Shannon—"

"Yes?" At his deep tone, her heart, which had only just slowed, started to beat quickly again.

David shook his head, changing his mind, and reached out to trace her bottom lip. "I'll be in touch," he told her.

Shannon stood clutching her flowers while he walked away from her. Yes, he would be in touch. The question was, would she be ready?

Markey looked up from the hose he held as David Courtney came into sight and got inside his car. He'd observed Courtney with Shannon long enough to realize that whatever they shared personally didn't need his prying eyes anymore.

He'd meant what he'd told Shannon. The cop was a good guy. He was ashamed again that the promise of money—and the memory of an outdated kindness—had made him a bad guy.

Shannon had always supported the community, believed in doing what she could with her center to meet its needs. He hadn't realized just how much until he'd come to work for her only a few days ago in an effort to get closer to her. When he'd called her out of the blue to ask for work, she'd obviously been surprised to hear from him after so many years. But she hadn't hesitated to help simply because he needed something and she had the power to give it. Peter LaCrosse, her dead husband, had been the same, generous like that.

Conversely, what had the man he took orders from ever done that deserved the allegiance he'd so unquestioningly given? He was a street punk. Jerard Booley had been one too, and look where he had ended up. Poor, discarded, and dead.

And the man who'd pulled their strings was still getting rich.

The truth was, Markey Shaw would most likely still be wandering the streets if Shannon hadn't given him this job and the respectable means to soon rent the first place he was going to be able to call entirely his own. She'd risen far above him in the world, but not for a minute did she remind him of it. That was the Shannon Davis he knew, had always known. And he had forgotten.

That's why he'd decided it was not going to be too late to make amends, even if she didn't know it. She'd given him a place to start: Martin Hanna and Tom Pierce. He knew where to ask around for the answers that would do her some good.


"How long has she been hanging around Courtney?" Arnaud threw back the last of his whiskey while he gripped the phone.

At the other end of the line, the Iceman's attention was caught by his opening study door. "Hang on," he murmured. "What is it? I'm on an important call."

His wife answered, "Yes, I know, dear. But our guests are important, too. You've been gone for a long time."

The Iceman curbed an impatient retort. "Five more minutes."

His wife backed out the door, shutting it behind her.

The Iceman said to Arnaud, "Shaw says he's convinced all that's between them is a personal thing, though we both know there's good reason to suspect more. She has too much history with us."

"Dammit, why now? Two more weeks is all we need to finalize the deal. After that, all of the La-Crosse money will be in place. Shannon—*no one*—must interfere."

The Iceman knew that tone of voice, understood what it was asking. "I'll take care of it."

Betty Morris hung up the kitchen extension a shocked second after her husband. Dear God, what had Parker gotten himself into? Her unsettled gaze touched the fine china and crystal and silver and art that accented the room she'd spent a fortune to decorate.

What had he gotten them *both* into? She left the kitchen, pasting on her bland hostess smile. How was she going to get through the rest of dinner? She knew she wasn't going to get through this night without finding out to what extent her husband had lost his mind.

The gray-suited businessman who had pretended all evening to be a banker in the Morris's home thanked his hostess for a wonderful meal and left.

He drove his tasteful sedan downtown and used his access card to get inside the parking garage of his building. A tunnel to the main-office network spit him out into the brightly lit corridor. He walked briskly now.

With luck, he could file his report in time to still make it home to tuck in his kids and hold his wife. Thirty minutes later, he shut off his terminal for the night.

As he drove out of the garage, he smiled at what his hosts' reactions would be if they knew their guest was really an undercover special agent for the real federal enemy closing in on them.

# CHAPTER FOURTEEN

It was just going on ten-thirty when Shannon heard the soft knock on her apartment door. She sat where she was for a moment, feeling her heart race, then settle. She laid down her book and uncurled her feet from beneath her ankle-length robe.

She didn't need to peer through her peephole to know who stood on the other side.

David stood leaning against the doorjamb when Shannon opened her door to him. His hands were in the front pockets of his jeans. He appeared to be giving great contemplation to his sockless feet, which she suspected he'd hastily shoved into the expensive loafers he wore.

In fact, everything about him looked slightly mussed, as if he'd moved quickly before he'd lost his nerve. Shannon smiled a little, and stepped aside, letting him in.

David walked to the middle of the room, still with his hands in his pockets. He said nothing as he took in the soft, pastel furnishings of her living room, which he'd only glimpsed briefly once before.

"Pretty," he finally commented before he turned around.

Shannon stood where she was, not knowing exactly what it was he wanted her to do. She lifted her hand to tug nervously at a short strand of hair at her nape. "Do you want something to drink?" She made a move toward her bar and never got past him.

David reached out to gently grasp her slender wrist. With a little tug, she was facing him. In silence, he tracked her lovely features, pausing to consider the frown line that marred her smooth brow, the question that hovered in her deep brown eyes.

At last, he confessed, "I didn't want to come, Shannon. I almost didn't."

She would have stepped away, but David didn't let her. "Then why did you?" she whispered.

David looked at her, feeling the full weight of resignation he had been struggling with all day. "I think I may love you."

"David—"

He didn't give her the chance to say any more. He framed her face with his hands and merged his mouth with hers, breath to breath, sigh to sigh. Shannon whispered in his ear where he needed to go.

Once there, he faced her beside the bed, breathing in her scent, taking in her warmth. Soaking in the pastel prettiness she'd surrounded herself in, and that he knew was completely in character with the Shannon he was coming to know in his heart.

When she lifted her hands to the tiny satin ties of her robe, David's were there to still them. "Let me," he said, and gently untied them. The garment parted to reveal a low-cut gown that cupped her small breasts as intimately as he wanted to do.

But he forced himself to wait. He wanted nothing about this night he had waited for forever to be rushed. And so he backed away until his legs touched her bed. He thought about muting her lamp, wondering if she'd prefer him to. But the banked flame he saw in her eyes as his hands went to the hem of his cotton pullover told him she wanted it on, too.

The hardest discipline Shannon had ever known was to stand where she was, passive, while David undressed. She'd felt his unspoken request to take the lead in this when he'd first kissed her. And in that moment, she'd also understood his desire for more. It was a craving for a total experience she shared.

And so as he finally came to her nude and aroused, like some sleek, stalking beast, she stood acquiescent, burning to let him take her wherever he wanted them both to go.

David pushed the robe from Shannon's shoulders. It drifted to the plush carpet on which her gown soon followed. He lifted her in his arms and lowered them both to her bed.

Shannon found his skin was warm, and its texture both thrillingly smooth and hard to her touch.

When he would have kissed her, she forestalled him by touching his nape and the clasp that held the waving silk of his hair.

When the length of it was free, she let it envelope her fingers, then she lifted it a little and let it sift back down so that the curling ends could tingle the tip of her tongue.

David shut his eyes and arched a little when her mouth moved to his throat. He felt the nibbling sensation she bestowed all the way down the length of his spine. He shivered, then lodged a reciprocal bite against her shoulder until she was trembling, too. That made him smile.

Shannon's soft little exhalation tickled the hair on his chest when he cupped her breast and leaned down to kiss her there. She thought she heard him whisper, "I love you," just before he straddled her and she braced for his deeper caress.

Her small fists closed around his smooth shoulders as he found her and began to press home. When he was as deep as he could go, she raised her knees up to hold him closer. His hair-dusted legs gave delicious friction to the smooth counterpoint of her own.

She was so soft, so sweet, so perfect, David thought. He groaned a little, feeling all of the sensation of his longing pool hotly where they were so intimately joined.

Suddenly, Shannon arched as he continued to move, and David knew he'd never seen anything more beautiful or heard anything more alluring than her breathy little call of his name.

They moved together slowly, languorously, then more urgently until he felt his climax building. Shannon's blunt nails indented his skin too delicately to hurt, but more than enough to erase his control.

"Oh, God," she breathed, "oh, God . . ." His thrusting intensified until she cried out and went still against him for mindless moments.

Even as she fell back against the pillows with a shuddering sigh, David felt her inner pulsations stroking him madly still . . . again . . . again . . . until he went rigid with ecstasy and groaned.

He was still coming down when he felt Shannon's hands sifting through his hair. He gathered enough strength to caress her shoulder with his tongue, then he disengaged himself and tucked her quietly against his side.

Minutes sifted by. Their breaths calmed. Their bodies started to cool. "What are you thinking?" David wondered if her answer would help him find his own.

He'd never experienced any physical encounter this intense, but hesitated to tell her so. The moment was heavy, and he didn't want her to think his response to it was trite.

"I'm thinking that I want to hold this night close to me for a long time to come," Shannon told him. She didn't tell him she was also thinking what they had just shared couldn't possibly have been so complete for her if it hadn't been tempered with the beginnings of love. Real love, not the simple desire she'd once convinced herself was the only emotion she felt for him.

David didn't voice any more questions and Shannon didn't volunteer any more answers. Neither wanted to disturb the aftermath with introspection that would come soon enough tomorrow.

"David?"

"What, honey?"

Shannon opened her eyes, still a prisoner of the netherland between dreams and waking. Her room was dark now, only the pale glow of the moon spilling through the slats of the louvered shades. She forgot what she'd felt drowsily compelled to say. Instead, she marveled at how the dim light limned the golden body above hers, gave a glint to the long, dark hair that touched his shoulders.

Still hazy with sleep, she felt overwhelmed by the shadow-and-light beauty of him as he moved to love her again. Shannon raised her hands to his shoulders, kneaded them with a circular caress. The beauty above her shivered and braced himself on his knees. Prepared to savor, Shannon went still.

Caught somewhere between sleep and waking, she let her hands wander down his powerful torso. They met briefly against his toned buttocks where she squeezed, coaxing a little grunt from him. Then she changed direction and meandered to another sensitive spot.

When her warm fingers closed around him,

David had no breath left. Every memory of earlier sensation that had roused him to turn to her again lay vulnerable in the hard-soft heart of him she began to stroke so tenderly.

When she curled her other hand around his neck to draw his mouth down to hers, he came willingly. And when she punctuated the madness she was wreaking on his lower body with a deep, open-mouthed kiss, he didn't realize his own hand dropped to join hers, to help her, until her soft thighs parted, inviting him back home.

Dear God, she felt even tighter, hotter, wetter, this time.

"Do it harder . . . harder . . ." she whisper-chanted.

Helpless not to comply, David felt himself rushing once again to the delirious brink.

His orgasm was a heartbeat within reach when Shannon gasped deeply and her body arched. Her head turned sharply into the pillow beneath her.

David followed her down that lightening road of sensation, crying out as his body poured into hers. It seemed like forever before his heart slowed enough to let him lie still.

This time, he didn't separate their bodies. Rather, he kissed her deeply while his hands trailed to her breasts, and his fingers rubbed her nipples, still sensitized from his loving.

He held her until she quieted and drifted back down into deep sleep. And as she did, he found he was trembling anew.

Incredible, he thought. Supremely contented, he closed his eyes and let sleep claim him, too.

When he roused next, he turned his head to find Shannon already awake. She was staring at the window, watching the dawn approach.

David turned from his stomach to his side and pulled her back against his chest. He needed to touch her. From the way she willingly snuggled into him, she needed, just as badly, to be touched.

"There were times when I wanted to die," she said in a voice so low, David had to strain to hear it.

Oh, God, honey, he thought, sensing what was coming.

"When they locked me in that place, I was so humiliated, so scared that I'd never get out that I just wanted to die." Shannon turned her head enough to meet his eyes. Hers were very serious, very sad, still haunted. "You know I'm not speaking figuratively, don't you?"

"Yes." His answer was as stark and grim as her quiet confession had been. This woman lying against him, hesitantly opening up to him was not the being of joy and light who had made magic with him last night. She was the dark, guarded woman prison had taught her to be.

"When those women beat me, when they had me on the ground hurting me so badly, I thought I really was going to die."

David felt a helpless rage. In that moment, he wanted to exact a painful revenge on who had put her there himself.

"But worse than the pain was the realization that after a point I just didn't care. I had nothing. I didn't have Peter, I'd lost my life's accomplishments, my achievements. I couldn't even hold on clearly to the memories of the hope I had so painstakingly created for myself."

David felt her tears drop onto his hands and slide over his wrists.

Shannon whispered, "The dark was the worst. Every night, before sleep came, I was back on Ernst Street. I was Shannon Davis, locked in an airless, cramped closet I could never escape from. I was trash life was never going to let amount to anything no matter how hard I tried.

"Oh, David, you can't begin to understand that total despair unless you've been there."

There was nothing he could say to that, to take away her pain. And so he pulled her closer, trying to imbue her with some of his strength. He kissed her temple and absorbed her quiet sobs, intent on making her believe that the past was gone. Determined to make her understand that for as long into the future as she wanted him, he would be here.

Long minutes later, after her tears stopped, David still hadn't found words that were more adequate than the physical bond her sorrow and his comfort seemed to have forged. Finally, it was Shannon who broke the quiet.

"Thank you," she said, her voice still husky with grief.

"For what, love?"

For wanting me, she thought, for believing in me. "For holding me," she said.

"I'll always hold you if you let me."

Shannon closed her eyes, feeling tears well up again. But these were not tears of darkness. They were tears of joy and maybe for the first time in a long time, tears of healing.

When Shannon awoke to the full light of morning, David was gone. She felt an abrupt panic, then sadness, then resigned disappointment. She saw a small sheet of paper on the pillow beside her.

It's a brand-new day, and it's beautiful. So are you. I love you.

David

Shannon reread the words and pressed them to her naked breast.

*Oh, David,* she thought, moved, feeling a return of joy.

She thought of Peter. What they had so briefly shared had been real. But opening her heart to David had taught her something else. While Peter had been her love, her heart, from the very first, had recognized David as her passion.

And close behind that realization came another one. The threat Markey had warned her about was still out there, and it extended to David, too. She had to tell him what she knew so that he would be prepared if danger came.

Someone had already tried to kill her once. Now that she'd finally found David, she wasn't going to be responsible for his vulnerability too.

# CHAPTER FIFTEEN

Parker sat at his kitchen table, finishing his breakfast and the last bit of the morning paper. It wasn't easy. His wife had been alternately staring at him and brooding for the past hour. Surreptitiously, he watched her lift her cup to take another sip of coffee that had to be cold by now.

She released another heavy sigh.

Annoyed, Parker laid his paper down on the table with a snap. "What's wrong with you?"

"The question is, what's wrong with you?"

He frowned. His wife wasn't the most articulate person in the world, but neither was she usually terse. "What are you talking about?"

"Why didn't you tell me about this trouble you're into?" Then she covered her face with her hands and softly began to cry.

Taken completely by surprise, Parker said carefully, "You're not making sense. What are you talking about?"

"Don't sit there and lie to me. You know what I'm talking about. I heard you discussing it yesterday."

"Heard me—?" Now he was angry, realizing what she had to mean.

"I picked up the phone!"

"You eavesdropped," he murmured with cold fury. "*Damn* you, you had no right!"

"*You* had no right to jeopardize everything we've worked our whole lives for, this house, our possessions . . . what kind of game are you playing?"

He leaned across the table and said in his most conciliatory tone, "Listen to me. It's not what you think, but I can't explain right now because I simply don't have the time. We'll talk this over tonight. In the meantime, trust me when I tell you everything is going to be all right. I've always taken care of you, haven't I?"

Betty stared off into the distance, still fretting.

"Honey, do you hear me?" It was all he could do not to shake her into acquiescence. "If you say anything to anyone before I explain, you could endanger more than just our material possessions."

That brought her around.

"Do you understand me?" he insisted.

"Oh, my God, you mean this is something that could get us killed?" She squeezed her cup and stared down into its cold contents. She muttered, "Shannon."

"*Shannon?*" Parker took a mental breath, trying to absorb the second blow of the morning. What did she know, what had she put together? "What does Shannon have to do with any of this?"

"What?" his wife murmured, as if just remembering her husband sitting in front of her.

Parker scraped his chair back and came around the table. He clamped his hands on his wife's shoulders. "You heard me. I'm not playing. *Talk* to me *now!*"

His fury helped snap her back to alertness and cautious fear. "I didn't mean anything. What's *wrong* with you? Shannon's name was part of your conversation and I'm just wondering—I just don't understand what any of this *means.*"

Parker looked hard at his wife. Was she telling the truth? Abruptly, he let her go and walked to the kitchen door. He took his suit jacket off the coat rack, picked up his briefcase, and turned to look back at the woman who watched him. What was best to do?

"Remember what I said," he finally told her. "We're not in trouble. We'll work everything out. Tonight."

Betty didn't know how she managed a smile. When the door shut behind him, she got up from the table, feeling as if she were moving through sludge. A fresh cup of coffee in hand, she sat back down and tried to figure out what to do.

Perhaps he was right. He had always taken care of her, protected their life and everything they owned. She couldn't know for sure that his conversation really implied something truly ominous. Then again, she'd trusted him blindly about Shannon once before and, in the process, had helped to almost destroy the woman's life.

Even when that had so recently become clear, he had still shown no regret for what they had nearly done. That had caused her first real rift toward him in her heart. And now, with what she had just learned . . . that rift was widening.

Shannon, she thought again. She herself didn't understand what she'd stumbled into, but Shannon, who was finally beginning to trust her again, might.

Markey looked up from feigning repairs on his perfectly good bicycle tire just as Betty Morris walked outside her house and locked herself inside her car. She took off in a hurry and Markey swung himself astride his bike to follow. He found himself actually grateful for the crush of traffic that helped slow down his quarry.

The call to stay with her if she left the house, to report where she went, had reached him less than an hour ago. He'd listened to the calmly spoken words. He'd tried to reconcile their demand, his conditioned impulse to obey, with his newly conflicting loyalty to Shannon.

Shannon had proven herself his truer friend. She didn't deserve what was about to come down on her. If the woman he followed was setting herself up to be an unwitting catalyst for that, he needed to know.

And so he maneuvered between cars to get in closer to Betty's. His real motivation in following her, he decided, would be directed by his own intent.

He inched along behind her for a block or two before traffic broke and he had to pedal hard to keep up for about the next half-mile. When traffic clotted to slow her again, their speed stayed moderate all the way to her destination. He'd been right. They were at Shannon's apartment building.

He rode past Betty and swung smoothly around the corner a few buildings down, then got off his bike. He leaned against a low chain-link fence, peering around it every few seconds to see if Betty would go inside.

She didn't. She hovered, idling along the curb for long minutes. Then she obviously made up her mind and pulled away.

Markey didn't bother to get back on his bike. He had Betty whenever he wanted her.

Shannon was sitting right in the middle of a trap that Betty was about to set off. He couldn't go to the police about it because he was guilty of too much himself. He couldn't reason with his own men because they were too close to getting what they wanted and had already proven themselves completely ruthless.

With a weighty sigh, he climbed back on his bike and pedaled away. There was one thing—maybe the only thing—he could do. Had to do. *Shit.*

\*     \*     \*

Arnaud slammed down the phone. How could the lawyer have been so careless? He could still hear his pleading to let him take care of handling his own wife.

But he couldn't be trusted to do that now. He had jeopardized everything because of his failure to keep secret what they were doing. Parker's assurances that he could keep Betty in line no longer convinced him.

He thought of the overseas call he'd placed a couple of hours earlier. That was someone— maybe the only one—he could absolutely trust. And knowing who he could trust was imperative now. He was absolutely *not* going to take any more chances. And that meant with Parker, too.

David found the address he wanted and pulled up in front of a smallish square brick house. At the gate of the chain link fence surrounding it, he spotted a pit bull puppy asleep on the front stoop. He pushed the gate open just a crack, waiting to see what the dog would do.

It raised its head and growled a little, then it started down the front steps. It walked right up to the crack in the fence, barked once, then started wagging its tail.

David reached down cautiously between the crack, letting his fingers hover. Just as cautiously, the dog licked his hand.

David stepped through the gate, closed it, and secured it behind him. With the puppy as a curious escort, he walked to the front door and pushed the bell. While he waited, he noted the drawn curtains, incongruous with the warm summer sun that gilded the day. Automatically, he reached under his summer jacket to touch his gun where he'd holstered it.

The door opened, and the expression of the woman who peered out at him was no more inviting than the facade of her house.

"Mrs. Arnella Shaw?"

"Why do you want to know?"

"Markey," David answered succinctly.

"That crazy boy—is he in trouble again?" Even as she asked, Markey Shaw's mother scanned the street behind him. Seemingly satisfied that he was alone, she stepped away from the door. David followed the dog inside.

"Shannon, you got a minute?" Markey hovered in the doorway of her office.

Shannon swiveled her chair completely away from the window, leaving behind her thoughts of David. "Come on in. And shut the door," she added," guessing by his expression that they might need privacy.

After he pushed the heavy door shut, Markey took one of the visitor's chair. "I've been doing some asking around about the guys you asked about. Something's turned up. One of your boys drew a blank but the other one is still very active right here on his old stomping ground."

Impressed at how quickly Markey had been able to get results, Shannon folded her hands on her desk. "Tell me."

Markey told her that for years Martin Hanna had kept his ties to his community strong in interesting ways.

Hanna had grown up in a neighborhood not two blocks south of this center. The connections were extramarital pursuits. They pulled him from his wife and children and his highly respectable corporate existence into a nearby hotel twice each month.

"He pays a couple of girls to make him happy in ways I'm sure his wife couldn't even imagine."

"I see." Shannon leaned back, contemplative. "So what of it? What does that have to do with Peter?" Or Alan, or the LaCrosse Corporation, she added to herself.

"Hanna's girls talk. I'm sure he doesn't know it because if he did, he wouldn't keep dropping the little pillowtalk tidbits he does."

"Tidbits?"

Markey nodded. "They surprised even me. In the right hands, I think they could really cause some talk."

"Is that right, Markey?"

Both Markey and Shannon turned to the door.

"You should have locked it," David said, walking inside and closing it completely himself. "The wrong ears could have overheard and picked up something I'm sure neither of you want to get around."

"David," Shannon began, "I was going to tell you—"

"Yeah? When? After you got yourself hurt, maybe?"

She understood his concern, but she didn't appreciate his sarcasm. "You're not the only one able to keep business under control. But since none of us need to discuss the fine points of that now, let Markey go on with what it is he has to say."

"By all means," David said, turning to Markey. "Sorry I interrupted."

"That's okay," Markey murmured, looking from one to the other. "The bottom line is, Hanna is heavy into some big-deal European investments that I couldn't get too many details about. But the interesting thing that you probably want to know is that he's got a pipeline between here and those investors that would surprise some mighty powerful people he does business with here."

"Does that pipeline lead to Alan Quade?" Shannon ventured, not quite daring to believe.

Markey looked at her startled. "How did you know?"

Shannon shut her eyes. When she opened them, she saw David's concern reflected on his face. To Markey, she said, "I wasn't sure, I didn't know. Now I do."

Markey looked at her strangely then dropped his head, running a hand along his jaw.

"There's just one thing with that, Markey,"

David said from across the room. "Something I want to know."

Markey frowned. "What?"

"Where did you get your hat?"

Markey looked blank for a moment. "What?" he asked again, weakly this time.

Shannon looked from David to Markey. "He's my friend," she said to David. "He's yours too; that's why he's come here to help."

"You heard me," David answered mildly, ignoring Shannon.

"David—"

"I don't know what you're talking about," Markey tried.

"Bullshit. That logo on the bill is literally one of a kind, right? Did you take it as a souvenir, as a reminder of a job well done before or after you helped Alan Quade 'die'?"

Betty locked the back porch screen behind her. She was no closer to an answer about what to do than she had been after Parker had gone to work.

She needed to get out of the house, to think. Maybe the anonymous company of the downtown tourist crowds would help her think it through more clearly.

Securing her fanny pack around her waist, she juggled her keys in her hand and headed for her car, parked along the deserted, tree-lined curb. She had her key in the lock when she heard a motor rev behind her.

Crazy kids, she thought. She unlocked the car,

got in, and started the ignition. The explosion rattled several windows along the entire block.

By the time one of her frightened neighbors pushed aside her curtain to investigate, Betty Morris and her car were consumed by a bright ball of flame.

"Damn," Markey muttered.

"Precisely," David echoed. "Why don't you tell us about it?"

"Is it true?" Shannon's voice was chilly. In the space of seconds, Markey had become another friend who had betrayed her.

"Shannon, I don't know what to say to you," Markey tried to explain. "This isn't like it seems. I really wanted to help you."

"Before or after you tried to shoot her?" David tossed out.

Markey's eyes shifted.

David started across the room, "You son of a bitch!"

Shannon was around her desk with her hand against David's chest before he could get to the cowering man. Somehow she managed to speak around her own rage. "Tell us the whole truth, Markey. Now."

Resigned, Markey talked.

Much of it, the personal stuff, David had learned from his mother just this afternoon. It had brought him rushing over to the center where he hadn't known, until Arnella Shaw had told him, Markey was working. He'd been angry with Shannon for not telling him, more with himself for not staying on top of Markey enough to know.

Markey told them how his mother was a long-time "friend" of Alan Quade's—or more accurately "lover." He explained how when he was a child, he had been treated by Quade, on those rare occasions that he'd visited, like a surrogate son. Not a real son, his mother had insisted, though Markey had never really believed her. Gifts clothes, money—nothing had been too elaborate for Quade to bestow on the boy.

But then, his mother and Quade had drifted apart. Or rather, his mother had finally gotten fed up with Quade's indifference whenever he wasn't in her bed. She'd barred him from her house one day after she'd barred him from that bed.

But Markey, now a streetwise teen, hadn't emotionally cast Quade out and Quade knew it. He'd exploited the boy's affections a few short years later when he involved himself in business machinations that required eyes and ears on the street. Markey's eyes and ears. His goal, he told Markey, was to discredit Parker LaCrosse's wife. And Markey had played along, just glad to be a necessary part of Quade's life again.

"He used me to recruit Jerard to harass you," Markey continued, ashamed at the hurt he put in Shannon's eyes. He turned to the cop, better able to withstand his disdain.

"Quade never fully explained why he wanted me to help him in the boating scheme, and I didn't ask. His money was coming into Mama and me when it sure as hell wasn't coming from anywhere else.

"I got to Millenak the night before he did. He and Parker Morris—"

Shannon glanced at David.

"Yeah," Markey confirmed, seeing the exchange. "He's in it, too. Deep. Quade and Parker had already scouted out a sight miles away from the marina where Quade planned to rent his fishing boat that day. I was the most scared about it. Afterwards, I couldn't believe we'd pulled it off."

Markey explained that Quade had been thrown from his boat near a tiny cove he'd been headed for. Markey, who had been waiting there for him all morning, saw him, and he'd rescued him. Then, under the cover of the cove, Markey had pulled Quade into his own boat—Parker's boat—and it had been a simple matter to hide Quade from public view.

Markey and Quade, roughly the same build, had traded garments in the shelter of the cove. Markey had stuffed Quade's cap in the pocket of the oversized slicker he wore as concealment over the other man's clothing. After that, Quade had simply to wait until the early morning hours to disappear into tragic obscurity.

"Obscurity where?" David demanded.

"Paris. He operates there under the name Arnaud. But he's not the only one." At David's frown, he clarified. "When he and Parker were planning out how they were going to embezzle money from Mr. LaCrosse's corporation and then transfer it into the European hands it needed to be put into, they worked out a code.

"In the beginning, to keep all their communications simple, they agreed that all foreign calls placed here to Parker in the States would be issued by a French businessman named Arnaud. If anyone on Parker's end became suspicious about the frequency of his conversations with the Frenchman, the manufactured cover existed in France and would withstand prying eyes.

"Before Alan got to Paris, their Parisian Worldcom contact used the name. Afterwards, Alan assumed it when he took over as Parker's contact there."

"Jesus, Markey." Shannon was overwhelmed that the self-effacing young man she'd always thought him could have been such a willing party to all of this deviousness.

Markey shook his head, as if he hadn't heard her. "And now, after all of that, I give myself away by wearing his hat." He was too embarrassed to admit he held onto it for sentimental reasons. He couldn't pretend not to know now the full extent of what Quade was. But deep inside where he never allowed anyone else to touch, he still thought of him first and foremost as the father he'd never had and had always wanted.

Shannon's phone rang.

"Yes?" she murmured. Her hand tightened around the receiver. With a quiet, "Oh, my God. Okay." She hung up.

"What?" David demanded from his chair.

Shannon looked at him, then Markey. "That was Parker. Betty's dead."

David shot a look at Markey. The little man hung his head.

# CHAPTER SIXTEEN

"Parker, calm down." Quade held the phone to his ear and, with his free hand, tilted the decanter of wine to the glass in front of him. All concern, he listened to Parker's panic, then insisted, "How could you even think I'd have anything done to Betty?" Someone else had—beating him to it. Markey? If that was so, the shooting episode with Shannon demonstrated more than impulse. It showed an instinct he'd been underestimating by confining the boy's talents to surveillance.

"That's your grief talking, my friend," he placated Parker. "Just listen to how irrational you sound."

Parker Morris leaned back against the plush folds of his easy chair. He closed his eyes, struggling for restraint. His wife was dead. He knew what his friend was. "Of course it's my grief, Alan," he lied. "I'm sorry, I don't know why I'm attacking you like this . . ."

"I know this is hard, and I know this is going to sound callous. But maybe in the long run it's for the best."

Jesus, it had to be a test. Parker waited for whatever else Alan would say.

"My concern now, my friend, is for you." Alan told him. "Are you sure you're going to be okay? Can you function the way you need to?"

"Of course," Parker answered tersely. "Don't worry, I've come too far to risk screwing it all up now. It's just going to be hard to accept Betty's death."

"I understand. She was my sister, too, you know. Take it easy. Rest for a couple of days. I'll be in touch."

Parker waited for Quade to hang up first. After the connection was severed, he reluctantly made a decision.

"Were we wrong to let him go?" Shannon leaned back into David's arms. They were sitting on her sofa and it was late into the evening. Their confrontation with Markey had happened hours ago, but the sour taste of it still lingered.

"Markey isn't going anywhere we can't find him, Shannon. We know too much about him and he's practically confessed the rest. I'm letting him stew a bit longer because I rather think he's in a key position to help us."

"Meaning what, exactly?"

"Neither Morris nor Quade know that he's turned against them. That means he's still a confidant and therefore a valuable resource for us. We can use him if we have to."

Shannon thought it over, that and much else,

especially the toll Alan Quade and Parker Morris's quest for Worldcom had taken on so many.

"There's another thing," David said. "I've got contacts with the FBI—"

"Like the IRS?"

David smiled bitterly. "The one I probed about Worldcom's real corporate identity revealed in confidence that I wasn't the only one curious about the corporation. It seems Parker Morris has been under covert federal investigation for some time on suspicion of embezzlement."

Shannon sat up.

David pulled her back against him. "After Markey's revelations, that's all become public." David told her he'd also learned other people in federal corridors, interested in the investigation and its suggested ties to Worldcom—including European Worldcom counterparts—had grown suspicious of Alan Quade's death.

"Why?" Shannon asked.

"Because of the sudden corporate acumen Morris seemed to have acquired following Quade's demise. His strategies and management style had been, shall we say, startlingly reminiscent of his immediate predecessor's."

"So why haven't the authorities made a move on Parker?"

"They've lacked hard evidence that could take their inquiries from speculative to verifiable. I'm betting that with Markey's input now, much of that is going to change. In fact, I've already been in touch with my contact, who is very interested in talking to us."

And as if on cue, Shannon thought, her doorbell rang. She looked at David and uncurled herself. At the door, she gasped when she saw who stood waiting.

Parker Morris was no less startled to see the cop materialize behind her.

Shannon didn't realize she took an involuntary step back. David laid a reassuring hand on her shoulder. "What do you want, Morris?" he demanded.

Parker looked back at Shannon. "To come in. Are you going to let me?"

Shannon didn't budge.

A bitter smile touched Parker's mouth. "I take it what I have to say to you isn't going to be news."

"What do you want to talk about, Parker?" Shannon was barely able to look at him through her loathing.

"Betty," Parker answered simply.

Shannon reached back to take David's hand. When he squeezed it, she stepped aside to let Parker in.

He walked across the room to a wingback chair and sat down. Shannon and David returned to the sofa.

Morris looked at them both. "Quade killed Betty, or rather I'm sure he had her killed." He scrubbed his face with his hands.

Shannon gave David a look, then said to Morris,

"No, he didn't, Parker. Markey Shaw rigged it all on his own with a pipe bomb. He said he did it to thwart Quade. It was *because* of Alan that she and Jeff, and somehow Peter, had to die. Isn't that right?"

Morris stared at her for long moments, then his expression closed. "That's in the past. Regrets no longer matter," he told her coldly. "What matters now is that I tipped Alan off. *Dammit*. I panicked and told him Betty knew I was involved in something illegal.

"I told him it had to be only a matter of time before she thought about the other voice on the phone and recognized it. I never though Alan would move on her that quickly." He made a disgusted sound. "But then, according to you, he didn't. It was the kid."

"Was it always the kid?" David asked. "Has Markey always been the one to do the dirty work for you two?"

"Yes," Morris responded in an almost offhand way. "Usually. If not Shaw, we both had contacts among organized sources."

"Like Martin Hanna?" Shannon demanded.

Morris stared first at her, then at David. "Well, well. So you two know about him, too."

"I guess we've been a little busy," David said. "What I want to know is, why in the hell have you come to Shannon now, ready to confess all of this?"

"Because I know Quade," the lawyer answered. "I know how his mind works."

Shannon interrupted. "What you're saying is, he wasn't all broken up over Betty's death. Now you're scared he's going to come after you next."

Parker smiled humorlessly, giving her his answer.

Quade let Parker's phone ring for an eighth and final time before hanging up. It was late enough. The man should have been at home.

Quade mulled over his decision to reevaluate Parker's worth. The two of them went back a long way. Maybe that counted for something; maybe he owed Parker a reassessment of his loyalty before he sanctioned drastic measures. He thought for several more minutes before steepling his hands beneath his chin. There was a way . . .

When Shannon's doorbell rang a second time within the hour, the man she had originally expected to show up was on the other side. At David's assurance, she stepped back to let FBI Special Agent Ted Sampson walk inside.

"I don't believe this," Parker commented from his chair. "The other night at dinner, everything I discussed with you, our American Worldcom 'contact'—you were a set-up. It was all a lie."

"As you see," Sampson confirmed. "Now I guess that means we can start being straight with each other about the real facts. I think candor is definitely your best option from here on."

Morris looked away from the agent.

"In exchange for some very comprehensive information, Mr. Morris,'' Sampson said in the wake of Parker's silence, "maybe we can deal."

"Right, as if there were a maybe about it." He peered over at Shannon. "As you've implied, my life is on the line."

The three of them talked long into the night. By the time Morris and Sampson left, a strategy had been reached.

Parker felt sure Quade would try soon to contact him again. He suspected that though Quade was fully capable of living with the idea of having Morris murdered, some twisted code of fairness would probably urge him to give his colleague one last "chance."

Sampson had suggested letting Quade incriminate himself on Morris's phone, which could be tapped. A carefully maneuvered conversation on Morris's part could provide hard evidence of Quade's crimes.

Parker had agreed. Shannon, however, had raised the point that Quade, given his suspicions about Parker, wouldn't fall into that obvious a trap.

She had suggested, instead, that she be the one to draw him out.

"We have to bring him back here close to me, right here on his own turf," Shannon had insisted. "Only then will we have our best opportunity to corner him and take him. There's a way to make him nail himself by his own admissions and lies."

David watched Shannon pace from where he

sat on the sofa. He was damned lucky. Flawless beauty and the brains, courage, and determination to equal it.

Shannon's alternate proposition was simple. She'd appeal to Quade's ego to draw him in. "I'll prepare a series of notes with just enough detailed references about his maneuverings in Europe—I'm sure Martin Hanna will be happy to supply them—to convince him I know he's alive and why.

"I'll tell him all I want from him in order to stay away from the authorities is money, periodic payoffs to ensure my silence.

"Most of all, I'll want him to make that first payment to me face to face, so that I'll know he intends to deal in good faith. His ego won't let him resist that bold a challenge. He'll come."

Sampson considered. "Of course, by the time he hands over the money, the mere fact that he actually showed up to do it will be evidence of his wrongdoing."

"Yes."

"No." David came to his feet and stood in front of Shannon. "We know we can't trust him, Shannon. He's proven that, and although your plan is clever it's too dangerous. Alan Quade is a snake. Something could too easily go fatally wrong."

She hugged David, wanting him to know that she appreciated his concern. But a moment later, just as deliberately, she drew back to look deeply into his eyes. He needed to see as well as hear the conviction behind what she was about to tell him.

"I love you." She smiled at the quick pleasure in his eyes, realizing this was the first time she'd actually voiced it outside her heart. "I do, David, but this thing with Quade is between me and him. And it's long overdue. That's why this decision isn't yours to make."

David opened his mouth, then closed it again at Shannon's implacable look. He knew he could present a strong argument against what she proposed, using his concern for her safety as the sticking point. He also knew with the admission she'd just made that now he could use her feelings for him against her, get her to back down for his sake, to appease his concern for her.

But beyond all that he also understood that she was right. He really had no say in this final act against Quade because it deserved to be hers. What she had to do was for her sake, but because that was so, it now was also for their sake.

He kissed her softly, a little sadly, and reluctantly let her go. He comforted himself by promising that whatever the logistics demanded, she wasn't going to walk into any lion's den of Quade's making alone. Not as long as he breathed.

With Sampson's help, they set a plan. Shannon would write her letters. Parker would tell Quade that he'd questioned Markey and learned through him that somehow, Shannon definitely seemed to be on to them. He would persuade Quade that she was a time bomb. Until they could have her defused before she caused real damage, their best option was to appease her.

Before the week was out, Hanna talked, giving them what they wanted. He revealed names, places, and dates that strengthened the tie between Alan Quade and Parker Morris and Worldcom. By the end of the next week, Shannon was parceling out her letters. Two days after that, Quade contacted Parker Morris.

"I want her dead," Quade barked. "I want you to take care of it. *You* personally. No Markey, no other middlemen. You tell me you aren't feeding her the information, but I'm not sure you aren't lying. If you're telling me the truth, her death at your hands will be the proof."

Parker almost recoiled from the lethal intensity emanating from the man, even from a continent away. "Be reasonable, Alan. If you don't trust Markey to handle it, we have others eminently more skilled than me in coordinating an execution."

"I don't want others to do it, I want *you*! I should have had that bitch killed in the very beginning when she first started twisting Peter's mind, bending his will to hers."

"I'm with you, Alan. Listen, just tell me what you want and I'll take care of it immediately."

"She wants me to meet her face to face. She actually thinks she's a match for me." Quade laughed. "Well, if she wants a confrontation, she'll get one. She wants her first installment of money at Peter's summer house? Fine.

"She's never going to see that money, but what I'll see is her blood soaking the floor, Parker." He gave a hard sigh.

Parker could hear him regrouping and waited.

"If you won't pull the trigger yourself, you've got to move quickly to get a man who will. I'll be there to meet her in Virginia two days from now. You've got to have the details for the hit on her all in place by then."

"Who do you want?"

"That's your concern, but I want someone we both know. I want to be able to recognize him, to see that you haven't put some imposter in place to set me up. I want to meet a proven killer at that house so that I'll know you're as committed to everything as you say, including Shannon's death. Consult Hanna for direction if you have to. He's always come through in the past."

"I understand."

"She's never going to see that money, Parker. And I'm going to laugh over her goddamned corpse."

Parker assured Alan he'd arrange for Shannon's killer to be positioned inside the house before Quade arrived. While Quade moved out of sight to await the execution, Shannon would arrive and walk smoothly into their death trap.

"Good, then," Quade sighed. "Good."

After Quade hung up, Morris did the same, counting on the deal Sampson had promised him in exchange for his cooperation. He picked up the phone again and dialed.

Sampson listened carefully and made the counterarrangements with Morris that would put his own federal men in place to intercept Shannon's execution.

Markey hung up the phone feeling numb. A final order, Alan promised, just this final thing to be done and then they'd be free of Shannon. Everything would be back on track. Markey could even leave the country to live in France if he wanted, Quade said.

Markey looked down at the semiautomatic pistol resting on the table in front of him, thinking about what Quade had just told him one more time.

Markey was to be the safeguard to the assassination plan. He was, Quade told him, the only one he could trust. No one would know that Quade had arranged for Markey to show up at the house early, to let himself inside to hide a day in advance with a duplicate key Quade would provide.

And if everything with the hit man went as planned, fine. But if for some reason Parker reneged, Markey would be there to take care of it instead and all still would be well.

Markey sighed. If he was going to go along with Quade, he had to decide to do it now. Sampson and the other authorities had already put him through an initial questioning. It was only a matter of time before the cops decided to formally arrest him.

Markey touched the gun, caressed its barrel while his mind wandered. So this is what it all came down to in the end—Shannon's life or Alan Quade's. He dropped his head in his hands, sick with the knowledge that one or the other would have to die.

It was barely dawn when Shannon, David, and Sampson stood on the perimeter of Peter La-Crosse's Virginia estate. FBI agents were positioned throughout the grounds' extensive tree-lined shadows.

Quade, surveillance had informed them, had already entered the house. Sampson checked his weapon. David did the same, noting Shannon's look of apprehension despite her determination to go through with this.

Sampson said, "He's sure to be watching for you from upstairs, Shannon. According to Morris, that's where he intends to be until after he hears the shot he thinks has killed you.

"That's why I want you to be very careful when you get to the house. We've got you covered, but Parker Morris's hired killer doesn't know that. Timing is going to be critical to apprehend him while we keep you safely out of his sight."

Shannon moistened her lips with her tongue, which felt incredibly dry. "I understand. I'm to wait outside the front door long enough for Quade to get a nice long look at me. Meanwhile,

David and your men will enter from the rear. After three minutes are up, I'm to walk inside the foyer and await your next instructions, which will come from the study where you'll have taken the assassin."

"That's right. Now don't get anxious over those three minutes, you hear? We need that time to move into place to take out the killer. If he gets the slightest glimpse of you before that happens, things could get a little dicey real fast."

"You mean if I make a misstep—" Shannon began nervously.

"None of us is going to come out of this hurt." David's tone was harsh, but he gave Shannon and Sampson an encouraging look. Then he gripped his pistol more tightly. "Let's do it."

They moved.

At the front of the house, Shannon paused at the door, according to plan. She reached inside her purse, appearing to fumble for her key. Surreptitiously, though, she glanced at the illuminated dial of her watch. One minute gone. Two . . . three. She unlocked the door and walked inside.

From the bedroom that still held childish keepsakes he'd valued long ago—it seemed like a hundred years—Alan Quade settled back on the bed and crossed his legs. Markey sat silent and uncommunicative in a chair across from him. His eyes were closed, but Quade knew the boy wasn't asleep. The emotional distance worried him; he'd never felt it before. Truthfully, he'd never thought that he'd care, but he somehow did . . . no matter, he'd concentrate on Markey when this was all over.

He thought back just moments ago, when he had stood at the darkened bedroom window, looking down at Shannon as she let herself inside the house. Supremely confident of the outcome here, he was already savoring his return to Paris, his new life there and all the prosperity it promised.

He glanced at his watch. Two minutes since she'd come inside. Unconsciously, he tensed, waiting. He looked at Markey again and almost started. The boy's eyes were no longer closed but fixed intensely, hotly on his. Quade's eyes moved back to his watch. Thirty seconds, another thirty, another minute down . . . the gunshot rang out, making him jump.

Quade closed his eyes and smiled. He heard Markey shift but stayed as he was, savoring the relief he felt. Then he heard Parker's man steadily climbing the stairs. Belatedly, some instinct urged him to say, "Markey, get inside the closet for a minute; there's no need for you to be seen here."

"Do you know what you've done?" Markey whispered.

Annoyed, preoccupied with the final details of this hit that he had yet to take care of, he snapped, "Do as I say, you damned fool!"

Markey's head jerked back as though he'd been slapped. Quade turned away a moment later, missing something that went dead in Markey's eyes before he complied.

Quade watched the closet door shut, then walked away from the bed and over to the bureau where he'd set the satchel of money. It held the amount he and Parker had agreed on as the price on Shannon's head. Quade thought no payday would ever seem this sweet.

His back was to the door when he heard the assassin pause, heard him hesitate just short of opening the door. Then the door opened. With his smile still in place, Quade turned—and froze.

David enjoyed the supreme satisfaction of seeing the man before him look first at his gun, then around the room, as if seeking some escape.

"Too late," David said, shaking his head. "I'm afraid, you arrogant bastard, that this time you're well and truly caught."

An inarticulate sound of fury escaped Quade. "That *bitch*," he snarled.

"Yes, that bitch, Alan," Shannon said from the doorway. She spared David the briefest glance before walking inside to stand just in front of him. "That bitch has outwitted you, hasn't she?"

"I see," Quade laughed sardonically, noting how Shannon reached behind her, seeking David's hand. "I suppose now you think you're going to live happily ever after, is that it?"

They were all startled when Markey swung open the closet door. The hand that gripped his pistol swung quickly to Shannon, where he held it unwaveringly. "No, that isn't it," he announced. "Drop your gun, Courtney."

"Markey, listen—" David began in a low, calm voice.

"Goddammit, *you* listen! I said drop the fucking gun, *now!*" He took a step toward Shannon.

David dropped it. Shaw was completely out of control. David prayed his backup was as close behind him as they'd planned. Then Markey surprised everyone again. He swung the gun away from Shannon to Quade. David stepped in front of Shannon.

Quade, seeing the cold yet frighteningly determined look in Markey's eyes, stumbled back a step. "What are you doing? What do you think—"

"Shut up." Markey snapped. He held the gun steady while some spark of emotion touched and slowly transformed his face. A tear rolled down his cheek. "Just one question, one. Are you really my father?"

Quade started to answer, but hesitated. His gaze moved past Markey to Shannon, who stood frozen behind David. They seemed to wait every bit as breathlessly as Markey. He turned his eyes back to the boy.

"*Are you?*" Markey demanded again.

How dare he, Quade thought, furious. How dare he threaten him, disrespect him like the common street trash he was. Ignoring the faint emotion that had briefly softened him at Markey's heartfelt question, he crossed his arms and answered with a cruel smile. "No, I'm just the first man your tramp mother ever took in who pitied you. Looking at you now, God knows why."

Markey shut his eyes briefly. Through his closed lids, a second tear followed the first, then a third.

Sensing the opening, Quade took a step forward. "Give me the gun, Markey," he ordered, his voice commanding. "You're making a fool of yourself."

"No," Markey whispered, while Quade took another step toward him, then another. Within arm's reach, Quade stopped and Markey watched him, letting him come near.

From across the room, Shannon whispered, "My God." Standing side by side, the resemblance between Markey and Quade was startlingly clear. How could she ever have missed it, especially these last few weeks when Markey had constantly been so near?

"Give me the gun, Markey," Quade said, the defeated look in his son's eyes causing him to reach out to take the gun. He actually had his hand on the cool metal of it when Markey's eyes lost their fear.

"No!" Markey shouted.

Quade grunted, turning the gun away from himself a split second before it fired.

Markey still gripped the gun as a stunned expression crossed his face. He looked down at the weapon, as did Quade. Both saw the blood soaking their joined hands, and then Markey's grip faded and he dropped to his knees.

Almost at the instant of Markey's shot, the feds

and local authorities pounded up the stairs. David, his own gun back in his hand, pushed Shannon to the floor and yelled at Quade, "Drop it! *Now!* Drop it now!"

Quade looked at him, at the entering authorities and their drawn guns, and then back at Markey's weapon as if surprised to see it still in his hand. It fell from his fingers and clattered to rest beside Markey's bloody chest. Quade dropped to the floor and gasped as though he'd been driven there by a blow. "Markey," he rasped into the suddenly quiet room. "I'm sorry," he said almost wonderingly. Then with more force, he repeated it, "Son, don't—"

With his dying strength, Markey reached a hand up toward his father.

The authorities moved in then and dragged Quade, who still looked stunned, to his feet.

David turned to Shannon. She had crossed her arms over her chest and was holding herself tightly while tears ran down her own face.

"God, honey, don't . . ." David pulled her to him and tucked her head beneath his chin. He absorbed her convulsive shudders, guessing that what she was feeling went beyond what they had just witnessed.

"Too much death," she whispered against his neck. "Jeff, Peter, me, Markey—God, I thought I wanted to see him suffer . . . but I *know* that pain, David, I've felt his pain." She anchored her arms around his shoulders and pressed herself more tightly against him. "Just make it stop. *Please.*"

"I will," David soothed. He tangled his hands in her hair and let her cry, let her release the last of the pent-up poison this final needless death had wrought. "I'll make it stop," he promised. "Forever. Do you hear me, Shannon? I'll make your hurting stop forever."

# EPILOGUE

Shannon laid the lilies she clutched against the cool green earth covering Peter's grave. She glanced from it to the wreath she'd placed against Jeff's headstone, which stood close beside his father's. She took a step back and looked at them both, lost in thought.

When David took her hand, he moved close enough to let his arm encircle her. She felt close enough to him that she could stand here and openly grieve in his presence for another love that had been taken from her. And for a friend.

She'd lost them both because, in the end, neither they nor she had been able to trust enough in one another's integrity.

She wrapped her arm around David's waist, returning his support. She wouldn't make the same mistake twice, not when she'd miraculously been given another chance.

"What will happen to Quade?" she asked softly.

"Embezzlement, conspiracy to commit murder, dozens of other crimes the authorities are uncovering every day." He shrugged. "It's this year's trial of the century. But when it's over, the truth of it will be that Quade and Morris are going down hard. For a long time. Worldcom is already finished. Its ties to questionable money and illegitimate sources are too strong. They're all out of your life, Shannon, believe that."

She didn't say anything for a long time, but reached inside an outer pocket of her purse to retrieve her sunglasses. She savored the warmth and brightness of the summer sun that shone down on her and David as she took his hand and gently led him away.

"It's funny," she finally said as they walked, "but ever since that day Markey died—almost since that moment, actually—I have felt free of them." She tilted her head up to look at David. He was watching her—intently, she sensed—even though his own dark glasses shielded his eyes.

"It was like everything that had happened to me and those I love created this bitterness and this hate that wouldn't go away, but that filled me all the same . . . When I saw Quade's pain, a father's grief as it turned out, it didn't heal me as I'd always imagined it would. It was just human pain and it sickened me, made what I'd suffered seem fresh all over again." She shuddered and squeezed his hand. "Living with that kind of hate is no good. You can't beat it, David. You can't win."

Still watching her through the concealment of his glasses, the line of his mouth grim, he lifted her hand to his lips. Shannon reached out to cup his jaw as his kiss brushed her skin. She smiled. "I'd much rather live with love," she murmured.

David didn't answer and they resumed walking. Uncertain at his silence, Shannon glanced up at him after a bit to see that a corner of his mouth had lifted. She pulled a little on his hand. When they stood still, facing each other, she asked quizzically, "What?"

"I was just thanking God that you'd rather live with love. Because so would I."

Shannon smiled fleetingly before she grew solemn again. She leaned into David to kiss his chin. As if that were some signal he'd been waiting for, he suddenly reached out and pulled her to him, holding her fast, tight. It was, Shannon thought, as if he were making a memory of the moment to savor into the future. When she pulled back they walked on, their hands firmly joined, into the sunlight.

# DEAR READER:

During a recent trip to Washington, D.C., I was struck by two things. Much about the city truly is as beautiful and glittering as any eager city tour guide will tell you. But that iconic image of our nation's capitol is but one small portion of a very diverse urban pie.

The dichotomy between wealth and poverty—between political movers and inner-city jaded—is evident and profound. Shannon, David, and the conflicts they face in *Final Act* were born of my observation.

When they realized that human decency, respect, and hope for the future gave them a common ground more compelling than their differences, they were able to find their way to love. I'd like to think their discovery is a metaphor we all might share.

My next novel pits two FBI agents against one another.

Sean Alexander, a legendary field operative, finds his career close to tailspin following an unlucky twist of fate. Jennifer Bennett, his closest rival, sees her chance to surpass him in the wake of his failure. Their common enemy, a desperate kidnapper and the child he holds, is the catalyst that forces Sean and Jennifer to examine what matters most to them beyond pride and professional honor. Watch for their story in the winter of 1999.

I love to hear from my readers. Please write to me at P.O. Box 44378, Indianapolis, IN 46244-0378.

Until next time, peace and love.

Tracey Tillis

# EERIE SUSPENSE

# FEAR IS ONLY THE BEGINNING